MY NAME'S JOHNNY POPE

MILL CREEK JUNCTION SHORT STORY COLLECTION 2

J. A. BOUMA

EmmausWay
PRESS

INTRODUCTION

I've cut my teeth as a fiction author writing action-adventure thrillers in the religious conspiracy vein. With teams unraveling mysteries threatening the Church and the world, complete with global stakes, gunfights, and the obligatory car chases. I love those kinds of stories; love writing and reading them.

Yet sometimes I like to stretch out on the couch with a good mystery that's a bit more of a slow burn with a guy trying his best to bring a dose of justice to the world. Not in the global, conspiratorial, high-stakes-big-book sense of things. But in smaller ways, for one person or family or small town.

For a while, I'd been kicking around the idea of creating a fictional smallish town in West Michigan for several months, thinking it could be a fun way to tell the stories of real people living life while exploring faith, taking a page out of Stephen King's playbook with Castle Rock, Maine, and John Grisham's Clanton, Mississippi.

Then the Great Pandemic of 2020 hit, and it seemed

like the perfect time to kick off the project! After all, I was stuck inside like most people with lots of time on my hands. Figured I should keep busy, because as they say: idle hands are the devil's tools! Sounded like great fun anyway spending my new-found time with a new set of characters in a new world outside my normal world that had been blown up by a crazy virus and the story world of my existing fiction.

Thus was born Mill Creek Junction, as well as a host of characters—like Jonathan Aquinas Papadopoulos. Aka Johnny Pope. He was the character I'd wanted to take things slower with my storytelling, doing something on a smaller justice scale with stakes that hit close to home.

As you'll soon discover, Johnny is a former priest turned private eye. After several decades serving his Mill Creek Junction parish, hearing their confessions and connecting them with the heart of God, he wanted to more intentionally fight for justice than what he was able to behind the cleric's collar. It was a way for me to explore some of those kinds of themes and some of the pain that comes from the brokenness of the world—in big and small ways.

Here is the first collection of five original private eye short stories with Johnny at the center. There's a variety of stories, from gritty true crime to more action-packing thriller to a mystery involving crop circles. Because when you're a PI freelancer like JP, you never know what assignment you'll encounter! Especially when your main client is Gideon O'Donnell, the small-town lawyer who functions as his boss. Along the way, you'll meet some more characters in the Mill Creek world that will give you some entertainment, while offering a dose of inspiration along the way.

Visit www.millcreekjunction.com for more details about the world and to follow the lives of real people living life and exploring faith over the coming series of stories—including the P.I. exploits of Johnny Pope. It'll be worth it, I guarantee!

Grace and peace,
~J.A. Bouma • July 2021

MY NAME'S JOHNNY POPE

MORE OFTEN THAN NOT, life comes at you like a two-by-four; sometimes a Mack truck. When it does, coming at you with a left hook that lays you out on your backside, I might be your guy. Ya never know.

Then there are other times, though, when it dribbles down from the heavens with a splat of bird crap on your eyeglasses. Right before the pigeon careens out of your blind spot, made all the worse by the high-noon sun comin' at ya bright and comin' at you at a blinding angle right before the dang beach bum claws those eyeglasses clear off your face, right before peckin' your eyeballs clear out of your sockets.

And when it does, I'm definitely your guy. I do charge a steep price. A pretty penny, as the kids used to say. But I'm worth every bit of copper.

My name's Johnny Pope. And I'm your only hope when life takes a crap on your eyeglasses, right before you lose both eyes to a pigeon you never saw coming.

Strike that. I'm the guy who takes care of the thing you never knew existed.

And if I'm offering my services, I should be honest: Johnny Pope ain't my name. Well, the Johnny part is. Papadopoulos is my given name. But Jonathan Aquinas Papadopoulos doesn't roll very well off the tongue. And besides, let's be honest: Jonathan Aquinas Papadopoulos just sounds like a pretentious prick. Like some East Coast yuppy who stepped off a hundred-foot sailboat—or rather, sailing yacht the kids call them nowadays—donning Sperry loafers, tanned bod sporting a pair of loose-fitting khaki shorts and a plaid Polo shirt of bright oranges and reds and yellows and blues donning a faded yellow sweater with said Polo logo in navy draped every-so rightly across his shoulders.

It also doesn't fit too good on a business card, and most people can't pronounce it to save their life, let alone spell it or remember it. Which ain't too good for the line of work I do, when fellas and felines alike need a name at the drop of a hat to clean up the pigeon crap and get their glasses back, maybe get a few stitches or an ounce of justice after their eyeballs have been clawed out of their sockets.

So Johnny Pope it's been the past decade since I set off on my own after leaving my previous profession that inspired my *nom de plume* in the first place.

I sat down with my coffee at the bay window over-looking a dreary Main Street morning. Not my normal cup of Joe, and didn't much care for the corporate brew, but it worked.

Black; no cream, no sugar, and definitely none of that

hippy bottled crap—vanilla this, caramel that, and that cinnamon dolce other thing that screams commie pinko to high heavens.

Which was a bit ironic, since I promptly unfurled my *New York Times* newspaper that was filled to the brim with them blowhards. But hey, man's gotta read what the men of his day read if he's to stay one step ahead of the enemy. Been fighting them ever since Nam, and then in the priesthood after that. But that was a former life.

Strike that—former *lives*. In service to both the State and the Church. Politics and religion. As one can imagine, I'm not all that popular at parties.

But that's another story, for another day.

Taking off my black beret and tossing it to the other chair at my table, I started scanning the headlines above the fold. Some nonsense about the knuckle-headed president tweeting only God knew what and nearly carrying our country to the starting line of conflict in a part of the world I continued to have nightmares about. At the third headline my phone buzzed at my leg. One of those dumb phones, made of plastic and with a lid that still offered a man a shred of dignity.

I ignored it till it went limp.

Until it didn't, buzzing up another storm a beat later that rivaled the one rolling in off Lake Michigan forty miles due west and threatening Mill Creek Junction with a mid-morning rain.

I reluctantly pulled it out.

Then wished I hadn't, squinting at the dot-matrix-like text scrawled across its face and throwing up the offending party calling way too early for my pay.

Gideon O'Donnell.

I frowned. Figured.

I let it buzz a few more times, popping the top to my grande Sumatra and taking a mouthful that did the taste buds good, flooding my senses with earth and herbs and spice. Better than I thought it would, that's for sure. Usually tasted like cardboard and gym socks, but today they scored a win.

Just before the thing went to voicemail, I answered it.

"Gideon O'Donnell," I grunted. "What a surprise."

"Where are you? What are you doing?"

I took an obnoxiously loud sip of my grande Sumatra, holding the phone up to my mouth as I imbibed, then I rustled my *New York Times* and held the phone aloft, capturing the hustle-and-bustle of the morning crowd.

I heard Gideon bellow for my name as I brought the phone back to my ear.

"Where do you think I am, genius? You know where to find me on a Monday morning. Hell, you could pop on over if you deigned to come out and mingle with us peons."

"Can't. I was called up on a case."

"Oh, yeah?" Another sip, another headline from that knucklehead with too much Twitter time on his hands making headlines that could flair up another conflict to rival Nam. "What about?"

"Arson."

I raised my head and looked out onto Main Street, the morning sun now shrouded by a threatening wall of shelf clouds, dark and stacked to Heaven itself, threatening nothing good. A fire engine ambled south. No lights, no sirens. Wondered if it was coming back from where Gideon had been called to duty.

"I need you, JP," he said, refocusing my attention.

I took another sip of my dark roast, then another before replacing the white plastic lid. Getting her ready for the road.

I sighed and folded the *Times* back into place, then again and slid it under my arm. "Figured as much when I saw you pop up on my caller ID. And on my day off, I might add."

"Sorry, brother. But I need you on this one. Could get dicey."

I stood and grabbed my beret, fitting it back on my head as he gave me the lowdown. I took my coffee up to the counter to top it off, the guy yammering on about a case that kept getting curiouser, then headed out into the crazy.

I was gonna need the full grande.

A rumble of thunder in the distance greeted me as I left Starbucks, a hot wind chased by a cool breeze whipping something fierce as I reached my F-150. A retro-style throwback model to the 70s I saw advertised down on a lot in Ohio. The kind from an era when Ford still knew how to make a pickup truck. Painted crimson with a cream panel ringin' the perimeter, fat tires with treads that meant business lifting my baby off the cracked pavement an extra few inches. Was a spittin' image of my first car, the one I'd picked out after gettin' home from Nam.

A drop hit me square between the eyes as I opened the cab door. Felt like a flashback to Nam and a near miss with the Grim Reaper when my platoon leader was smacked by a Viet Cong hornet standing behind me as I bent down to tie my shoe. Could have been me bleeding out from the knob on the forehead. Hell, *should* have been me bleeding out from the knob on the forehead. But the Holy Father had other plans.

I climbed inside the beut that reminded me of the one I got back from Nam after serving right up until they'd hauled our backsides back April 30th. Drove the original into the ground after settling back in the Junction and settling down. Then Lynn happened, then seminary and taking a post with my childhood parish, Saint Thomas Catholic Church after Lynn passed, and I traded my original heart's desire for an Oldsmobile.

Didn't know why I was thinking of her then, but I was smacked upside the head back to reality when another few water hornets smacked me in the face, then started soaking my shoulders and back, the static scent of rain and charged atmosphere filling my head until a crack of thunder shuddered through my teeth.

I slipped inside the cab and slammed the door, the rain really beating down now but the wind not carrying it far. Just a late-summer storm is all, the heavens opening up and letting loose, Noah's Ark style. It was gonna be one of those days; the rain seemed to portend it. And Gideon's phone call—a curious case, to be sure.

Roaring my crimson beut to life, I ambled down Main Street as another fire engine ambled back the other way, then another. Three in one morning heading back into town? I guess Gideon was right. It was that bad.

I flipped the station to WGRD, the local oldies rock station and caught the tail end of "Born to Run," The

Boss letting loose along with the rest of the gang and sending me back to an era I'd soon forget. In fact, I thought I had. But for some reason the past was surfacing in a way I couldn't escape.

I shook it off and focused on recalling my convo with Gideon, and the mess his client had gotten himself into. Which apparently had something to do with a previous case he'd just won.

Gideon's client, Jeffrey Peterson, a Mill Creek councilman, had been the talk of the Junction some months back after some auto parts store John got fresh a few too many times with his wife. Until the offended husband sliced and diced his wife's neck.

For posterity's sake, I should add *allegedly*, especially since the councilman who'd been caught drunk as a skunk on Main Street beat the rap on a not-guilty jury verdict. And now the store of said auto parts store John had been torched to high heaven and the councilman was facing new charges.

Arson.

Nothing official yet, and Gideon didn't even know if his client was being fingered. Wanted to get in front of it all just in case.

Hence Gideon's early morning phone call to the Junction's finest private investigator.

I took another sip of my dark roast growing cool, The Boss giving way to Queen, which suited the morning about right. Then I saw it, Burt's Auto Parts smoldering like some field after a napalm bombing raid.

It had been a good-sized warehouse, painted forest green on the sides stretching back half a football field with a few windows that looked like they were still standing. Brown brick faced out toward another main drag off the far end of Main Street where a bunch of big-box retail outlets sat. Not the big corporate type, but some locally owned joints, along with Meyers General and Happy Day Inn and The Green Thumb and the like.

I pulled up behind a remaining fire engine and rolled down my window. I raked a hand across my bald cap and whistled, shaking my head at the sight, feeling for Burt.

The arched roof that was normally covered in bird crap had collapsed in on itself, like someone had taken a fist to one of those old-school Jiffy Pop popcorn plumes, tearing a hole clear through and the smoldering remains of the inside belching black smoke and hissing something fierce and throwing up white steam from the rain picking up speed. A part of one side looked like it had collapsed inward, as well, leaving the joint a complete DOA loss.

A man with a clipboard wearing a faded yellow rain jacket caught my attention. He was head down, scribbling something fierce while some lackey in a Carhartt jacket held a large black gold umbrella over his head.

Billy Babcock. Local chief inspector for the fire department. Decent fellow who was thorough and fair, if not earnest with a bit of a stick up his rear. If he was working the case, this one must have gone right up the food chain at the butt crack of dawn.

Should be interesting...

I grabbed my own umbrella, navy blue with white, and unfurled it as I got out of the cab, those kamikaze raindrops rapping against the fabric something fierce. I hustled toward the man just as it looked like he was wrapping up, clicking a pen shut and stuffing it on the inside of his rain jacket before drawing his clipboard inside an open flap for protection.

Running up to him, I said, "Hey, Billy. How's it hangin?"

The guy didn't startle, but twisted his skinny frame around for a viewing. Then brightened into a knowing grin. "Johnny Pope! Figured you'd show your mug around here sooner or later."

"Oh, yeah? Why's that?"

The man shrugged. "Given the prime suspect is your boss's client and all."

I frowned and crossed my arms. Now that's interesting...

"First of all, O'Donnell ain't my boss. And second of all, where'd you hear one of his clients was being fingered for this?"

Billy took the umbrella from the underling and waved him off. "The Prosecuting Attorney's office nabbed this straight away, given the arson victim had a material connection to a case they just tried."

"*Alleged* victim, you mean? And how do you know it's arson?"

"Oh, it's arson, alright." The man pointed off toward the still-smoldering building and shook his bony little pointer. "Started in the back and raced forward along a line of accelerant before blooming up toward the roof and wreaking havoc."

I took in a measured breath and followed his finger, taking in the view. A part of the roof shifted, crashing down into the still-smoldering remains and sending up another protesting plume of smoke and ash and white steam.

I folded my arms and sighed. Just great. Accelerants meant only one thing.

Deliberation and premeditation. And more importantly: a human cause.

"Accelerant?" I said, acting surprised.

"Yessiree, Bob."

"Inside or out?"

"On the inside, running along the wall that collapsed over yonder."

I twisted up my face. "Then how do you figure my guy is the perp? Did you find any sign of forced entry, a busted window, or—"

"Hold it there, killer," Billy said, putting up a hand. "You can have your boss interrogate me to his heart's content on the stand in a few months. I've got paperwork to file."

Billy spun around and walked off, the rain really going at it now. Which would make my own job that much harder.

I watched him skitter off, disappearing into a minivan from the previous century.

I turned back toward the monstrosity gone belly up, with a gazillion questions on my mind that led to bad answers for Gideon's client.

There was certainly motive. The guy nailed his wife and left him with the bill. Opportunity was up in the air, although the client certainly knew who the perp was and where he worked; it had been the talk of town, after all, as well as had come up at trial. The weapon was an iffy proposition, but any accelerant would work; Councilman Peterson certainly had access to gasoline.

Yep. Things were definitely getting interesting.

Glancing behind me and around, I walked toward the auto parts store. Time to get to work.

I stepped over a line of yellow police tape sagging from the continued rainy onslaught. No one was around and figured I had a right to inspect the place given my client was about to get charged for the damage, if not already. The fire had been put out long ago, both from the Junction's finest on top of the morning storm gusting off from Lake Michigan.

I came up first to the front doors. Locked solid, without a trace of forced entry. Wouldn't peg the perp to have gone in that way anyhow, but you never know. Especially knuckle-headed councilmen embarrassed by the specter of an adulterous wife.

Finding most eyeballs having left, busied with other manner of work, I moseyed on around the side, glancing back again out of habit but finding no one interested in what I was doing. I edged around the corner and walked the length of the side still standing strong, despite the collapsed roof and most of the other wall hanging by a thread. I sloshed through wet weeds clawing at my thighs and avoided rotting boards and cinder blocks that looked like they pre-dated the fire, scanning the few windows that lined the wall and perimeter for anything amiss. Surprisingly, the windows I had seen at the start hadn't blown out, and they were unmolested. Which meant, again, no forced entry.

Same for the back. A rusted steel emergency exit

door greeted me, sealed shut. No lock or knob on its face. Which mean no one could have gotten inside through the back. I continued on across the back to the other side, where I was met by the wall with a serious case of palsy. It was broken in the middle, where it had collapsed, the cinder-block edges like teeth or puzzle pieces waiting to be put back together again. I kept going, nearing the front and finding another pair of windows that were completely intact. Not a scratch or scrap or crack on 'em. A minor miracle that did my heart a bit of good, knowing it would make my job easier painting the picture Gideon needed to clear his client.

At this point, I took out a small camera. Old school, I know, but the dumb kind of phone I carried around didn't do the job. The small Nikon worked just fine for what I needed. I snapped several shots as I made my way around the joint a second time, noting the front door, the side windows, and the back door with plenty of Kodak-moments to fill an entire trial. I'd sort through them later, but I wondered what good it would do anyhow.

Finishing, I made my way back to the front, the rain having died down to a mist. I climbed over a row of fallen cinder blocks piled all catawampus at the front, nearly careening over the edge to my death, and noticed someone across the street. A man, wearing dark jeans and a navy jacket, arms folded and leaning against a telephone pole while smoking a Camel. Who knew if it was in fact a Camel, but it seemed to fit the scene.

A weird fog stretched its tendrils across the pavement as the rain gave way to mid-morning and sun began heating up the world after the storm riding a cold front pushed past. The guy just stood there, watching the place and the remaining workers mop up, a faint glow burning bright right before a haze of blue left his parted lips.

There had been a few stragglers when I rolled up and thought I'd caught him earlier. Wondered who he was, what his interest was in it all. Whether rubbernecking bystander or otherwise interested party.

So I decided to ask.

Stuffing the Nikon in my jacket, I strolled over to the guy and pulled out my own pack of Camels, slapping it against my open palm and withdrawing a cancer stick. Yet another part of Nam I'd brought home with me. Knew the things would kill me sooner or later, but figured what the hell. Surviving the Viet Cong'll do that to ya.

"Got a light?" I asked, holding up the stick as I approached the mystery man.

He stiffened, sucking in a startled breath through his own stick, the end burning bright and a faint contrail rising into the sky. He looked up and down the street, as if he was confirming I was talking to the kid who looked in his mid-twenties, then nodded and withdrew a Bic.

I held the stick up to my lips and took the lighter from him. Flicking it to life, I inhaled then handed it back, nodding my thanks before gesturing toward the hollowed-out carcass of the auto parts store.

"Quite the blaze, eh?" I said.

He laughed, more a grunt than anything but bearing some teeth as his Adam's apple bobbed up and down on another chuckle—placing the response somewhere between amusement and disdain. Maybe both.

"You could say that," he said before inhaling, a stack of ash forming quickly as he worked his cigarette hard.

I took a toke myself, glancing at the patch at his breast that had come loose at one side, curling toward the center. A name tag. *Stevie.*

Gesturing again at the building across the way, I took a chance and said, "That your joint?"

"Me? Naw. Well, yeah. I mean, I didn't own it or nothin'. Just a worker bee."

I smiled. Didn't figure the kid for the entrepreneurial type, so his response was amusing. But interesting he'd shown up at the site, gawking for who knew how long.

"You know he was going under, right?" Stevie offered.

Now *that* was interesting.

I took another drag and shook my head, then blew the haze into the day growing sunnier and hotter and muggier now. I took off my jacket, my Nikon falling to the ground with a bounce. I cursed under my breath for the carelessness.

The guy startled and twisted up his face. "You a cop or something?" he said with a rush, voice jittery and that Adam's apple bobbing up and down again. He finished off his stick and flicked it to the curb.

I picked up the camera, praying it wasn't damaged. A dent but nothing major. I shoved it in my jacket and rolled it up, then stuffed it under my arm.

"Not cop. Private investigator."

"Like a private eye, investigatin' somethin' for someone?"

"Something like that."

"Who for?"

I drained the rest of my own cigarette and flicked it into the street as well, then stuck out my hand to redeem my misstep. Never throw off the equilibrium when a potential informant was inching toward the snare.

Which the Nikon had certainly done.

"For a client. A guy who might get fingered for the blaze."

He eyed me with clear suspicion.

"My name's Johnny Pope."

The man eyed my hand before taking it. "Stevie," he offered, leaving it at that, which was fine. I'd get the lowdown on the dude once I got back to my office anyway.

"I take it you work at the joint across the road."

"*Worked*," he corrected, lighting up another cigarette. He flashed the Bic at me and I took it, lighting up as well.

I chuckled. "I guess so, after the early morning blaze."

He blew out a white haze and shook his head. "Naw, man. Was canned a few days back."

My ears perked at that one. Disgruntled, canned employee, showing up at the scene of the crime? Very interesting...

"That's rough."

He scoffed and took another drag. "You have no idea. Found some shady stuff going down and started asking questions. A few too many, if you feel me."

"Yeah, I feel you. What sort of questions?"

"Why invoices weren't being paid, for one. Got some questions from our suppliers why we were behind on payments. I'm the supply manager, you see." There was a proud twinkle in his eyes before his face fell and he took another drag. He mumbled, "*Was* the supply manager..."

Tough break. And also interesting.

"Then when our paychecks were being delayed here and there, I started speakin' up for my co-workers. You know, the voice of the voiceless and all."

A regular Karl Marx, this kid was. But again, real interesting. Sounded like a major cash flow issue. Or more...

"So the way I sees it," he said, taking another drag before continuing. "The way I sees it, no way your client did the thing across the street."

I turned toward him, folding my arms. "Oh, yeah? Why you see it that way?"

"Because I saw this document on the chief's desk. Some legal filing, with something called chapter 11 typed up top."

I took in a measured breath, keeping my face flat but knowing my heart rate spiked at hearing those sweet words.

Because Chapter 11, the bankruptcy kind, gave Gideon O'Donnell the sweet words he needed to get his client off.

Reasonable doubt.

The mother lode. Which often came in the most unexpected of ways. Like a bloke leaning against a telephone pole smoking a Camel. But in my line of work, I took 'em as they came and didn't dare ask how I got 'em in the first place. Figured the good Lord was dispensing his mercies in extra measure that day.

And I was the lucky recipient. What was the verse in

the Book of Ephesians from the good Saint Paul? *'Blessed be the God and Father of our Lord Jesus Christ, who has blessed us in Christ with every spiritual blessing in the heavenly places.'* Different context and different meaning. That I knew from thirteen years of good parochial education at the hand of Saint Helen back down the road at Saint Thomas's. Didn't mean I wouldn't take such blessings when I could catch 'em.

Like a bloke leaning against a telephone pole smoking a Camel.

I nodded for the guy to go on. And he did, spilling his guts on tax filings he'd come across that didn't add up as I puffed away on my cigarette. Given his knowledge of the supply side of the business, he was in a position to have a pretty good idea of the cash flow situation. That, on top of the fact Burt was sniffing out Chapter 11 filings was all I needed to bring back to Gideon for the payday I'd expect from doing his investigative work.

I took my final drag and flicked the second butt to the street, the day really heating up now and feeling like I'd overstayed my welcome. I said, "So here's the thing. Would you be willing to go on record with all of this?"

Stevie's eyes got real big. As if I were the Secret Service pinning him down as a high stakes witness in some plot to assassinate the president himself.

"Uhh," he stammered, tossing his own butt to the street and lighting up another.

"There's money in it for you if you do. A consulting fee, of course."

He took a long drag, the end shining surprisingly bright against the morning light as the storm clouds gave way to sunshine. Probably from the sudden rush of dollar signs dancing in his head, like sugar plums before Christmas Day.

"How much?" he finally said.

I shrugged, not certain myself but knowing it would probably be enough to secure the confession. "Not sure, but I'll let you know once we get that far. You in?"

Another pull, another supernova at the end of his stick. Then he pulled out a piece of paper and pen and scrawled out his cellphone number.

Well, that was easy.

I made my way back to my office north of Main Street and spent the rest of the morning and the better part of lunchtime and the early afternoon combing my usual sites and sources for the lowdown on what might have gone down at Burt's Auto Parts. After compiling a goodly amount of intel, on top of what I typed up from Stevie's insights, I headed back into the heart of the Junction—right back to where I started at Starbucks, which was right next door to my main target.

Law Offices of Gideon, Winslow, and Seward.

I parallel parked the F-150 on Main and headed on in, the place finally back to a nice air conditioned coolness since a few weeks ago when the joint had been roasting in the late-summer sun. Something about a faulty condenser or something. Or so said Gideon. I made my way up the flight of scuffed wood stairs to the second floor and then to the office, where I entered.

Reggie offered a greeting before he returned to a copy machine. Lizzy was on the line but smiled and waved.

Gideon had been pouring himself a cup of coffee from a Mr. Coffee that looked like some Walmart special, smelling of Folgers or Maxwell House or some other sludge made from inferior robusta beans of most grocery aisle varietals.

I frowned at the sacrilege but kept quiet.

Gideon saw me and smiled. "Johnny Pope! My man, JP! Just the person I've been waiting for." He ushered me into his office, a cramped space that would feel far more spacious if he bothered to clean up the place. Books scattered about and manilla folders spilling their secrets made my head spin.

I was bearing a manilla envelope myself and slapped it on his messy desk.

"What's this?" he asked, picking it up and flipping through the papers.

"Your defense," I simply said.

He furrowed his brow and frowned as he scanned, his usual posture before his face softened and one end of his mouth curled upward.

He looked at me. "This is good. And this witness of yours is solid?"

I nodded. "Solid as they come. Which in my line of work ain't saying much, but it should be enough for what you need."

"Nice! Sounds like he'll throw some major shade on the original owner. Heck, maybe we'll Plan-B him."

I groaned. "Don't do that to the kid. He doesn't need to be fingered for this, especially since he's a willing witness. For our typical fee, of course. Besides, he got canned for uncovering what he did and poking his nose in Burt's business that's giving us what your client needs."

"There you go! We don't know he didn't do it. Getting canned seems like a great motive to me."

I sighed and folded my arms. Hated it when Gideon dragged people up on the stand, only to turn the tables and suggest they were the guilty ones who had committed the crime—whether we thought they did the deed or not, and especially whether or not we could prove it.

All in the name of reasonable doubt.

Gideon dropped his arms, the folder going with them until he tossed it to the desk. "You think Burt did this to himself? That he deliberately set the fire and torched his place?"

I shrugged. "Don't know what happened. But it definitely gets us the two words I know are music to Gideon O'Donnell's ears."

One end of his mouth curled upward. "Reasonable doubt."

"Case closed, then?"

He slapped my shoulder and grinned. "Case closed, partner. Or it should be. The illustrious Annabelle Kirkland is fixing to take this to a jury trial, and I doubt she'll budge, given her track record with our office of late. But you did good, Johnny. Real good."

"All that matters is that I get paid."

"You'll get paid alright. But what about the justice? You said you were into that sort of thing. The reason you got into the gig in the first place after things didn't work out at the parish."

I shrugged. "You, too, if I recall. And yet I didn't see you blinking before ol' Judge Heller, defending a man who slashed his wife's throat—not once, not twice, but three times."

Gideon frowned. "*Allegedly*."

I waved a dismissive hand and turned toward the door. "Yeah, yeah, yeah. So they say. I'll be seeing you, Gideon."

"Likewise."

Don't you know it, pal.

I walked out of his office, descending the set of stairs and out onto Main Street. Hanging a right and rounding back into Starbucks. Where this whole blasted day had begun, but now the sun was setting in a blaze of glory.

I ordered another grande coffee. This time a decaf. Caffeine did wicked things to my 60s-something brain, and I needed sleep after a long day. I picked up a discarded copy of the *New York Times* and sat at the table from earlier that day, tossing my beret back to its former seat and continuing where I'd left off almost half a day ago.

More often than not, life comes at you like a two-by-four; sometimes a Mack truck.

In the case of today, it was a can of gasoline and Bic lighter.

But when it does, when life comes at you with a left hook that lays you out on your backside—or a blazing furnace that shatters your life and threatens your freedom—then I might be your guy. Johnny Pope.

Ya never know.

BUT FOR THE GRACE OF GOD GO I

THE BREAKFAST CROWD was just winding down when I rolled up in my F-150, the vacant tables and just-finished ones mocking me through the large picture window to Millie's on Main at the heart of Mill Creek Junction.

About a quarter past ten and the day was nearly finished, as far as I was concerned. Couldn't believe I'd overslept my alarm. Must have hit it off instead of snooze, which was unlike me. But my wicked headache, compounded by a sinus infection was probably reason enough, even though I felt guilty for it and cursed my old sack of bones for needing more of the Zs than I'd ever needed before. Getting old sucked.

I'd prided myself as being one of those guys who was up before six most days. Usually around five, if I could swing it. Couldn't stomach letting the day go to waste on something as silly as the near-unconscious state of sleep. Never understood people who slept in, snoozing their alarms a dozen times until they finally mustered up enough self worth to drag their sorry rears out from under the covers to tackle the day.

Perhaps it was my Catholic guilt messing with me, the whole seven deadly sins a constant reminder of our fallen nature. Perhaps, but for me, a dyed-in-the-wool Catholic from birth who had once kissed the ring of Saint Peter as a mini Vicar of Christ just up the road from Millie's on Main as a priest, it was more than that. It wasn't just guilt, it was taking seriously the human propensity toward vice at every turn, and how easily our flesh tends toward vice when the lights go dark.

'And do not bring us to the time of trial, but rescue us from the Evil One' was part of the Lord's Prayer in Matthew's Gospel I prayed with the fervency of a Pentecostal. Yes, the irony wasn't lost on me. But still…I knew the Devil roamed the earth. *'Like a roaring lion your adversary the devil prowls around, looking for someone to devour,'* as Saint Peter himself wrote in his first letter.

And the morning was the Devil's playground as much as the night.

Sleeping in was gluttony compounded by sloth, pure and simple. And now it was a quarter past ten and I had Sister Helena bellowing in my ears from grade school.

Where was a priest when I needed one.

Oh, wait, that would be me! Or at least it had been me. Until I hung up the cassock and handed in my clerical collar. Sort of like a cop turning in his badge and gun.

A mug of coffee and a hot breakfast would have to do instead. I hoped it would assuage both the wicked headache and lingering Catholic guilt, but something told me not to ask too much of the Most Important Meal of the Day—even from Millie's fine fare, which was the best darn breakfast a guy could get in the Junction.

Putting the old dog in *Park,* I donned my black fedora and climbed out of the Ford's cab. Walking through the front door, a familiar jingle announced my arrival as a pair of working hands headed out. Probably to Warner Farms on the outskirts of town, where the historic windmill still turned sitting right alongside the Grand River amidst a sea of vegetables, giving the Junction its namesake.

Taking a deep breath, I smiled. Couldn't help it, what with the smell of freshly ground and brewed coffee saturating the air, compounded by melted cheese and frying bacon and baked biscuits and flapjacks that could feed the lumberjacks that had roamed these streets over a century ago when the town was founded. Suddenly, I was smiling and my headache disappeared, and I was in search of a good newspaper. Something caught my eye on a stretch of wood benches near the door that served as a waiting area. I picked it up and turned it over, then frowned.

A *USA Today.* It would have to do.

"Johnny Pope!" a familiar voice bellowed from behind. A shrilly, itty-bitty voice with gray curls and fair skin and killer red lips that surely melted the hearts of a few high-school quarterbacks in her day.

Millie on Main herself.

I turned around and grinned. "Mills!" I said, opening up my arms for a quick embrace. We did, and I continued: "You didn't have to throw out the red carpet for me, coming to greet and seat me yourself."

"Aww, I wouldn't have it any other way, seen as how you're my best customer and all. Wouldn't miss catching JP before I headed out for the morning."

"Best be careful, or Chet's gonna get jealous. And then I'd be in some serious doo-doo with the mayor himself on my backside."

She laughed. "Jealous? You wish, hot shot." She grabbed a menu and motioned for me to follow. "Your usual spot?"

"You know it."

She led me toward the back across the black-and-white tiled floor through the goodly space looking like a diner straight outta childhood. Basically preserved what had been here from before I was born when she took over the joint. Complete with chrome seats at a counter near the kitchen, baby blue- and pink-patterned booths along with steel tables and chairs. Which I much more preferred than the booths, right near the back at a big picture window along a side street jutting off Main back toward a neighborhood with turn-of-the century craftsman homes. In fact, the one where Lynn and I had first bought our own after Nam when we got hitched. Hadn't lived in it since she died and I left for the priesthood. And when I came back and got the gig at Saint Thomas's up the road, a parsonage had been provided on the church grounds that made the home up the road moot. Sold it and stashed the cash in an IRA that had been paying dividends ever since.

I sat down with the *USA Today* I'd swiped. Millie asked if I'd like the usual, eggs and bacon and unbuttered wheat toast, but I said I wasn't sure and she handed me the menu before leaving to fetch my cup of coffee. It was nearing eleven now, near midnight in my book. A tragic waste of the day, it was, sleeping in, the morning nearly over. Threw off my whole ordering scheme. But by the time she returned with a sufficient cup-o-Joe, black of course, I put in an order of eggs Benedict.

She scrunched up her face, making a sucking sound through pursed lips. "Sorry, darlin', but we ran outta ham."

"You ran out of ham? What kind of joint you runnin' here, Mills?"

"I know, sorry! We got the thinly sliced stuff for lunch, but we're plumb outta the Canadian-style bacon we normally use for the Benedict dish. How about salmon?"

I raised a brow and dropped my jaw. The day went from bad to worse.

Before I could object she added: "It's got cappers and a sprinkle of dill—"

"Sounds real interesting, Mills," I said with disappointment, then agreed and waved her off with a wink. She scooted on back to whip me up my eggs Benedict with—salmon. Who the heck ever thought ham should be swapped with salmon should be shot. Prolly some commie pinko from back in the East, or some commie pinko wannabe hippie from out West. Them types were always messing with a good thing, trying to progress what history had settled generations ago for some newfangled version that was less regressive, less offensive, less blah-blah-blah.

And yet, if anyone could mess with a good thing like

eggs Benedict, something I'd discovered on the West Coast before shipping out to Nam of all places, then it was definitely Millie on Main.

Still, I huffed out a muffled curse and shook my head, more an obligatory complaint from an old coot who was far too set in his ways to swap ham for salmon, than anything.

I unfurled my *USA Today* to dive into the day's news, while a Crown Vic with a mumbly, grumbly muffler pulled up to the curb just outside. It just sat there, too, some John in a hoodie just whilin' the day away inside. Like there wasn't anything better to do with the day quickly cresting toward midday than spoil an old man's late-morning breakfast with a mumbly, grumbly muffler.

Great. Now I had a two-pack-a-day broad in need of a lung transplant to contend with on top of the eggs Benedict sans ham.

Boy, did I sound like the grandpa on *The Simpsons*, or what? Old coot is right.

I took a breath and crossed myself, sending up a prayer to the Virgin Mary herself for another day of breath in my lungs to offer said complaint.

Amend that: *complaints*. Plural.

As if answering my petition, the Crown Vic gave up and cooled her jets.

Just as my eggs Benedict sans ham turned up, care of Millie herself.

"I know it ain't right, but I think you'll find it suits your style."

I looked at her, brow raised. "My style?"

She shrugged. "Old school with a side of sass."

I chuckled. "Sounds about right. Thanks, Mills. I'm sure it's great."

"You enjoy, and let me know if you need anything else, you hear?"

"Oh, I will!"

She wandered over to a table near the front to jaw it up with a couple of oldtimers like myself.

I stabbed my yoke, the yellow spilling over across my pink salmon that looked far too raw to pass health-department muster. But what did I know? Smelled alright, especially the buttery, lemony hollandaise sauce soaking the homemade English muffin the size of my palm. Cutting a piece of the bread with my fork and stabbing a piece of poached egg white and saucey-yokey-smothered salmon, I shoved a bite into my mouth.

When the door flew open with a smack.

And in strode Mr. Hoodie from the wheezing Crown Vic just outside my window, rushing inside and looking frazzled, darting his head this way and that, hands stuffed in the pouch at the front I always thought was a little too mammalian for my taste.

And sending the hairs on the back of my neck to attention.

Guy was white and average height, skin smooth and pallid and sallow, with wide, darting, icy blue eyes that bulged inside sunken sockets. Hair was black and long and stuffed under the hood but jutting out this way and that, with a weak showing on the upper lip that told me he was either just pushing into his mid-teens or was a twentysomething that struggled to grow a stache.

Either way, it sure was interesting.

And could get interesting.

Now, I'm no academy-trained cop. Never took any courses in law enforcement, and don't have the sort of street experience that would hammer and hone someone of higher law enforcement caliber than a mere PI like myself. But I've been around the block enough, before the priesthood and after—and frankly the priesthood itself taught me a thing or two to know when something ain't right.

Millie seemed to follow my brain waves on this one, taking hesitant steps toward the man as the couple she'd been jawing it up with a few minutes ago turned with curiosity. Two servers huddled behind the main counter in quiet, whispered discussion. As she approached the man, my stomach started tightening like a vice.

I set down my fork; the eggs Benedict sans ham would have to take a backseat to whatever was coming next.

From the back of the diner, I could hear Millie ask the man if she could help him.

Mr. Hoodie leaned forward, mumbling something to her.

Which made her recoil and ask, "What in tarnation?" with exclamation in a way that signaled nothing good.

Then he took a step toward her, one of his mangy paws sliding out of his mammalian pouch and latching onto her arm with force.

With violation and violence.

And that's when I stood.

Sort of automatic. Like I didn't have a choice. And I

didn't, not really. Not when Millie was being manhandled.

And that's when the other thing appeared.

A gun. Black handle, silver body, and a little pathetic. Some 9mm off-the-shelf peashooter kind of thing. Probably a Walmart special he had no clue about what he'd bought or how to use the dang thing.

Which meant he was more of a threat than the average John.

Someone screamed at the sight. One of the gals dressed in a pink lace dress behind the counter, her hands slamming against her mouth and sending a confusing jolt through the rest of the joint.

Mr. Hoodie took a sudden step backward and slammed into the door, the place shuddering with confusion along with the door itself.

"Just empty the draws like I asked!" he shouted, his hoodie slipping off as he stiffened with raised voice, a corkscrew vein bulging at the side of his forehead.

Which also meant he clearly meant business.

His outburst sent the girls behind the register into action, scuffling across the tiled floor and scrambling to meet his demands.

Millie shrank, hunching over with hands over her head and silver hair coming undone up top so that it fell over her face. I caught a faint sob echoing back toward me.

Which made my blood boil, hearing her like that and put under the gun. Literally, some pathetic 9mm Walmart rollback peashooter special aimed at her head now.

I wanted to retch at the sight. Almost did, the one piece of salmon working its way up on a geyser of hollandaise and bile and adrenaline that wondered whether it should keep pushing toward the surface.

It didn't, but the sight and sound of Millie pushed me to act.

I shuffled back a few steps to engage, my metal chair scrapped across the tile floor from the back of my calves. Nails on a chalkboard that caught the perp's attention up front.

He startled but didn't move, glancing back toward the scraping noise and keeping his aim on Millie as the girls at the two registers continued their task—the flaps holding down the Washingtons and Lincolns and Jeffersons slapping up and down, coins spilling on the floor with a tinkle from nervous hands.

I didn't move either, running my options through the wringer and sending up prayers to Mary and her Son and the saints for the strength and wisdom and fortitude to get 'er done.

Whatever that meant; however that looked.

Because sure as the grass is green, ain't nothing was gonna happen to Millie.

There was a sound near the counter. A plasticey, clangy *whoomp*, like a bag of groceries being hoisted on top.

In many ways it was; the perp's bacon was ready to be brought to whatever hellhole the guy was, well, holed up in.

"Go on," the man shouted, waving his Walmart rollback peashooter toward Millie. "Go fetch it fer me."

"Brother," I said before he could make a move of his own, "you don't want to do this."

My voice was strong and clear and resounding in the space silenced by the turn, communicating with clear conviction Mr. Hoodie had picked the wrong diner that morning to rob.

Suddenly, he grabbed Millie. By the hair.

She screamed and struggled, whimpered and wilted under the anxiety and pressure and violation of the turn.

Now I slide out from behind my table and strode across the waxed black and white tiled floor, my military boots offering up a squeaking protest as I made my way toward destiny before the perp could even process what was happening.

Then he grabbed her, by the neck. Arm around the front and cinched just above the collar bone.

Walmart peashooter pressed against her temple.

The worm had turned, as they say.

I stopped in my tracks, just to the left of the table Millie had been jawing it up at just moments ago—seemed like an eternity now. I was just past the main seating area and staring down the perp. Sixteen, eighteen feet away now.

I threw up my hands in a motion of surrender to let him know I was unarmed and not a threat.

Yet.

And that's when he threw me this look.

His eyes narrowed slightly; his neck craned forward with interest; his mouth dropped open with an inquisitive sigh.

Then his arm loosened slightly around Millie's neck,

and his face fell and drained a bit of color—what was left of it, anyway.

"Father Papadopoulos?"

He said it with an air of disappointment, almost embarrassment—even shame. As if the Almighty himself had caught him, arm clear in the cookie jar.

I had that effect on people from time to time.

I lowered my hands, then took a breath and swallowed, the faint call of sirens sounding in the distance now beyond the brick wall fronting Main Street.

Finally, Chief Roller and his county mounties were rolling up to bring this to an end.

But I knew better. This was far from being over.

And I was on the front lines of landing the plane.

The two of us stood still, staring at one another as Millie shivered and whimpered under the man's grip.

The kid clearly knew me from somewhere. Father Papadopoulos, he had said, a signal to a connection to my former life at Saint Thomas's.

I studied his face, eyes moving across those bulging eyes of his sunk in those deep-welled sockets. Moved to the hooked nose that narrowed to a point and his mouth of crooked teeth, a few gaps here and there. Then to the hunched shoulders and narrow, scrawny frame. Looked sickly, like he'd missed his last several meals.

He suddenly rubbed the underside of his one forearm holding the peashooter against his leg, a nervous, bothered tell that reminded me of my work with opioid addicts, their tracks flaring up for relief or more of the goods out of habit. Which also put two and two together for the rest of the man's appearance—the scrawny, sickly, gaunty, ghosty look about him.

Then it hit me. A familiarity about the man suddenly rose to the surface that placed this face with a name from a decade ago.

A teenager, from a large Catholic family in town—which I more than understood was sort of redundant—but a good, solid family. With Dad a CPA and Mom caring for the kids, keeping them on track with school work and carting them off to basketball practice and swim meets and dance lessons and concerts.

Never in a million years would I have imagined seeing that kid, from that family, standing in the middle of Millie's on Main, brandishing a Walmart rollback peashooter and robbing the joint while holding sweat Millie hostage.

Yet there he was, still staring a hole through me as the boys in blue rolled up, no longer blaring their sirens but still letting their reds-and-blues strobe under the high-noon sun.

Rick VanderMeade. That was the kid.

I blinked, then again and once more, as if trying to reset my eyes as I tried to make sense of what was in front of me. Little Ricky I'd called him back in the day. And there he was, holding a gun to sweet Millie's head!

"Rick, what are you doing, son?" I stammered. About the only thing I could think of saying in the moment.

A look of shame washed over the kid, his eyes averting my own and nose flaring and jaw clenching with emotion. Even the one arm still clenched to Millie loosened so that she slumped to the floor in a hysterical pile, the poor woman covering her head as she knelt, that muffled whimper returning.

Rick looked down at Millie then up toward the counter and around at the other patrons before landing on me again with those hollow, bulging eyes of his. Time seemed to stand still as he took in the place, and an almost realization seemed to hit him. As if he had just been wakened from a dream or some psychotic state and didn't know where he was or why he was there.

The man scratched his arm again, then said, "Needed the cash, that's what I'm doin'."

I took a breath. Alright. That was a start. At least he was talking.

Now Chief Roller was on the blow horn telling Rick to come out with his hands up. Went on about how he wanted to open up a conversation, and things didn't have to end badly, and a lot of other nonsense that didn't seem like it was from any playbook for such things. Although, doubt the Chief had ever contemplated being thrust into such a thing, so I should give the man some grace.

"What for?" I said, arms at my side and feet planted firmly on the floor, not moving a muscle for fear Rick would get jumpy.

He looked down to the floor and mumbled something, scratching his arms again.

"What was that?" I asked.

"For these," he said loudly, pulling back the sleeve to his hoodie and confirming what I had suspected.

The arm was littered with tiny mounds, darkened crimson dots anchoring the centers.

Needle tracks.

Wasn't proud of the fact I'd called it. Rick was a junkie looking for a fix. And needed cash to get it.

Millie's cash.

Which definitely wasn't happening now that the Junction's finest had showed up.

I went to offer a response when the man offered his own. "Coming back wreaked me, Father P."

I furrowed my brow and shook my head. "Coming back? From where?"

"Iraq, Afghanistan, you name it."

I understood what he'd meant. The man had had a rough go of reintegrating back into civilian life once he was finished fighting Uncle Sam's wars. Understood that well, given my own story.

"What division?" I asked, feeling like we were getting somewhere, all the while out of the corner of my eye I could see the Junction Blues preparing for something.

"82nd Airborne," he said.

Before I could react, Rick pulled down his hoodie to reveal black ink staining his neck that told the truth of it: two As, with an eagle underneath, signaling the 82nd airborne infantry division of the United States Army specializing in parachute assault operations.

I sucked in a startled breath, my mouth dropping a bit at the sight. For his unit was my unit from Nam.

"It was the damnedest thing, you know?" he offered, this look of wistfulness overtaking him as he looked at me, past me, off into a memory that explained what on God's green earth had happened to the kid I'd known from Saint Thomas's.

I cleared my throat. "What was?"

His head snapped back to me, and he drilled me with these eyes that told me there was a lot of chaos going on inside. He answered, "It was car doors and dogs barking and summer fireworks that started it all. Then some one would come up from behind, Ma or Pa, and I'd freak out on them from being startled."

Rick kept describing to a T what I myself had experienced coming back home in the summer of '75. Back then, they didn't have a name for what they call it now: PTSD. He went on to explain his only remedy for it all, which described to a T what I myself experienced. Opioids for him; bottles of Jack Daniels for me.

This could have been me forty-five years ago. But by the grace of God go I.

The Apostle Paul was sure right about that, a passage from his first letter to the Church at Corinth, chapter 15, coming to mind: *'For I am the least of the apostles, unfit to be called an apostle, because I persecuted the church of God. But by the grace of God I am what I am, and his grace toward me has not been in vain. On the contrary, I worked harder than any of them —though it was not I, but the grace of God that is with me.'*

I took a step forward now. Time to end this.

I sent up a prayer to the good Lord above, then said to Rick, "Look, son, I don't know your story. At least the one since you and I left Saint Thomas parish those many years ago. I don't know where you've been, what sort of roads you've treaded. But if that tat is any indication, I know how you feel."

Rick swallowed, his Adam's apple bobbing up and

down at the center of his scrawny neck. His bottom lip quivered some now and his eyes moistened over.

He managed just above a whisper, "You do?"

I nodded. "Nam messed me up something fierce. Didn't take to drugging, but drinking became my specialty. So while you might think you're the only one in the world who knows your troubles, you and me got a lot in common."

Rick's chest heaved a breath, and he let it out with a slow and steady sigh. As if the truth of what I'd just said made all the difference, just knowing someone understood him.

Then he said something entirely unexpected: "I would like you to take my confession now."

I almost said no, that I didn't do that sort of thing anymore. But I thought better of it. After all, I was still an ordained priest in the Roman Catholic Church, despite not having a parish to call home anymore. So I relented, moving on careful feet toward a man who seemed more than ready for the rite.

Reaching him, I took a deep breath, then said, "In the name of the Father, and of the Son, and of the Holy Spirit. Amen."

Almost on instinct, Rick went to his knees. Bowing his head, he responded, "Bless me Father, for I have sinned. It has been—well, years since my last confession. These are my sins..."

And there he went, unloading his confession of sins, including the one he'd just perpetrated against poor Millie and the others, taking her hostage and trying to rob her blind.

"For these and all sins of my past life, I am truly sorry."

Never got to the Absolution, or assigning a penance for that matter. In an instant, the front door flew back and a burly man led the charge of four more uniformed officers brandishing pistols and shotguns, yelling at Rick to get on the ground.

He did. Before long he was taken away.

I gave my statement of the events, recalling the details to Chief Roller as best I knew how. When the man was satisfied, he let me go, and I strolled back to my truck.

I opened the door and climbed in, a sudden hunger overtaking me. I chuckled to myself, realizing I'd never gotten past the first bite of my eggs Benedict sans ham. The salmon wasn't even half bad, now that I thought about it, the dill and capers that belied Millie's on Main, the Junction even, begging me for a second hearing. I'd have to get a second serving the next time I returned for breakfast. On time this time.

On time...

A thought rose to the surface. Imagine if I hadn't overslept and hadn't gotten a later start to the day. Might have missed the show entirely. Which might have left Millie in a more precarious situation than she had been with me grumbling about my eggs Benedict sans ham. Would have missed meeting a man from long ago who I had more in common with than I might like to think, ties binding us in a way that no man could understand, having gone through the hell of war and then the hell of life back home.

Yet also thankful just the same that the good Lord above had led me along a different path.

"But for the grace of God go I, is right," I muttered as I brought the F-150 to roaring life.

I threw her into *Drive* and pulled out on Main Street past a Junction police car, Rick slumped over in the back seat, and headed home.

STORY 3

A CHRISTMAS LIKE NO OTHER

IT WAS GOING to be one of those days.

One of those *Christmas* days. Which didn't surprise me in the least.

Made sense, given all the crazy this year. But it was more than that. Felt it in my bones when the second my feet hit the ice-cold floorboards, then when I didn't smell the coffee I'd set to auto brew the night before.

I'm not one of those guys who especially loathes the holiday. With a name like Johnny Pope (even if my full name is Johnathan Papadopoulos) and a background as a former priest, a guy in my shoes sorta can't exactly loath Christmas. No, it was more a feeling that was rearing its ugly.

Got turned onto it during the priesthood. Summer of '05 probably had something to do with that when I took part in the Exorcism and Prayer of Liberation course the Vatican opened to the two-hundred-fifty of us crazy enough to take them up on their offer. The last decade as a private investigator took that feeling and ratcheted it in a way even the priesthood hadn't. Something about the alignment of the strings in the universe or stars or something when the evils of this world manifest themselves through bald depravity clued me into when the world was off its axis, spelling trouble.

The strings were plucking a mean beat that morning, that's for sure. That cold floor clued me into that, and the fact my bungalow smelled of the crisp coldness of Lysol and not hot coffee. I wouldn't fully get how mean that beat was until the afternoon.

Truth be told, the downed trees on my street probably had something to do with that feeling things were off. Most of me blamed Mother Nature, but part of me blamed the Big Guy Upstairs, the Almighty having one last go of us this year. Although as a former priest, I couldn't exactly blame God for power outages. Didn't seem right, especially on Christmas.

But not only did I have no power, which meant no brew and breakfast but for a bowl of stale Cornflakes, the house was colder than Baby Jesus' manger! Worst of all, a major snowstorm had pummeled Mill Creek Junction overnight. And given it was Christmas, the power company wasn't going to get to flipping the switch back on any time soon.

Luckily, I owned one of those turn-of-the-century craftsman bungalows that's standard fare in the Junction, along with every other post-war Midwest town, complete with a modest fireplace in the living room that's mostly for show. But when God Almighty decides to drop a bomb cyclone along with a polar vortex, blanketing West Michigan with a foot of snow and ice and felling trees across the Junction, I put it to work. Dragged what felt like a quarter chord of conifer to keep me from dying of hypothermia. Had blown through half of it by noon when I got the call.

No, sir. No holly, jolly Christmas this year. That call came like this.

My living room was humming with the heat of my fire and a handful of Christmas crooners, the smoke and spice along with Bing Crosby and Nat King Cole making everything nice and festive. The Cornflakes didn't last long, so I made myself a PB&J and a cup of instant coffee I'd manage to scrounge out of my cupboard along with a mess kit to boil water from my Army-issued pack from Nam. Tasted like socks and cardboard, but it was coffee, and a throwback John Grisham paperback from the 90s made it taste that much better.

A tad.

Managed to make it to the inciting incident when my phone started jumping off the end table. Apparently, the cellphone towers hadn't suffered the same Christmas curse my coffee pot and electric range had. Lucky me.

"JP!" a voice yelled into my ear before I could even get a word in edge-wise. Wouldn't have recognized it had I not seen the caller ID.

Gideon O'Donnell, my boss.

Why the Junction's resident defense attorney was phoning me on Christmas morning, hadn't a clue. We were close, but not Christmas close. But the tone and tenor let me know my Junction Christmas had just been 2020ed.

I said, "Merry Christmas, chief, what's the—"

"No time for that now," Gideon said in a rush before sighing, as if he'd found his manners in his egg nog. "I mean, Merry Christmas, JP. Sorry to bother you, but we've got a situation on our hands. More like our clients do."

"What situation? Who?"

I heard him holler to someone about the difference between the accelerator and the brakes. That's Gideon for you. Sounded like he was rushing off to something, which wasn't like him. Must be bad.

"Sorry. Just get to Kenny and Barbara's place."

"The Robergs?" I said, voice echoing around my empty living room.

"That's right. You know them, then."

"Of course I do, but what's going on?"

"You know their house?" Gideon answered without answering. "Can you floor it there?"

I set my sock-flavored coffee on the end table and sat up. I did, and I could.

The Robers were your typical Mill Creek Junction family. Just had a newborn this past summer. Couldn't be more than four months old. Had the kid a bit into their mid-life—an oopsie, if I recall—with several other kiddos. The family wasn't part of my parish. Baptist, if I recall. Kenny worked at the community college in town, some-thing to do with business or communication, while Barbara played housewife. Not there was anything wrong with that in the slightest, just your typical Junction family, if not with a side of the 50s thrown in for good measure.

So the fact Gideon was beelining it to their joint like a madman on early Christmas afternoon and ringing me up...

The feeling proved true: It was going to be one of those days.

Scratch that: one of those *Christmas* Days.

I swallowed, mouth tasting of cardboard and dry from the ping of adrenaline as much as the coffee. "Give it to me straight, Gideon. What's the deal?"

There was a beat, then the deal: "Assault, JP. Maybe homicide. And no one's talking."

I closed my eyes and said a prayer.

He continued, "I'm on my way and—well, I know it's Christmas, but I could really use your help."

"Not a problem. I'll meet you in ten."

We ended the call, and I shoved the phone in my pocket. Thankfully, I'd let the fire burn down to embers. Not sure I'd have been comfortable leaving it burn down on its own with the way the day had turned from before my feet had hit the floorboards.

But, grabbing my stocking cap for my poor bald head, I jumped into my vintage F150, crossing myself on instinct after the thing sprang to life after a brief sputter, then eased out of my unplowed street onto Main Street.

Between the power outage and the morning murder, I considered the Christmas officially screwed sideways and was halfway to buying a ticket to Cancun. But I had a day to save. After all, that's what Johnny Pope did. When Christmas hit the fan, I was the one to sort the pieces and super glue it back together.

Not that I had anything better to do on Christmas anyway, my wife having died giving birth to our daughter I left at the Junction firehouse forty years ago.

But still...didn't make me happy in the slightest. Especially when the words Kenny, Barbara, and homicide were used in the same sentence.

Made it in eleven minutes, Gideon having already arrived. I parked behind him, who had parked behind a slew of MCPD cars still blaring their reds-and-blues. Thought it a bit much, especially on Christmas, but whatever.

I crunched across the leftover snow on the plowed driveway, a wind picking up across the flat fields that butted up at the backside of the single-story ranch. An ambulance was coming down the driveway, its lights flaring up now for a very good reason. Looked back as it passed me, but couldn't tell who was inside.

Whether they were alive or—

The other thing...

Couldn't wrap my mind around what had descended upon the Robergs, but I was about to find out.

Because Chief Roller was coming outside, lighting up a stick that didn't sit right. Last I knew, the man had quit. Which meant this must have been bad.

"Hey, there, Chief," I said, putting up a friendly hand and trying to grease the skids early on. The chief of Mill Creek PD and I weren't exactly on the best of terms. He sees what I do as less serve and protect as get-off and defend-at-all-cost. Can't say I blame the man. Would probably feel the same way if the tables were turned. But in the last decade, in my line of work, there were far more legal shenanigans on his side of the aisle than my own.

Chief Roller, a rotund man with an eight-ball head wearing a brown leather bomber jacket sporting the MCPD crest, leaned against the pulled garage door, cream paint chipping and dented from disrepair. He looked up and nodded. "Johnny Pope. Can't say I'm surprised. And actually not all that irritated."

Interesting...

Crunching across the packed snow, I stood in front of the man with hands in my coat pockets. He pulled a long drag before blowing out the haze of smoke and breathy steam toward the heavens.

The spicy, sweet tobacco made my mouth tingle with a desire nurtured in Nam. They handed those things out like candy. But I'd given up the bad habit after I married Lynn. And when she passed, I didn't go back.

He pulled out his pack and tilted it with an offer.

"No, thanks. Gave it up a while back."

The chief smiled before taking another long drag. "So did I."

We stood in silence for a moment, the wind moving across those barren fields with purpose now, a few sticks from naked trees falling and a passing car the only sound-track to our sorry Christmas.

Sighing a steamy breath, I went for it. "I'm about to go in and meet Gideon, so I'll find what I'm going to find either way. But, care to enlighten the unenlightened?"

Another drag, another spicy-sweet billow. Camels, if I had it right.

"What you'll find is a toppled Christmas tree, ornaments littering the floor. You'll find a stuffed Santa head —chopped off, with white stuffing fluff scattered about. Might even find some of that in the dog's droppings outback, for all I know." The man laughed and took another drag. "Saw the mangy mutt eating it like it was cotton candy. Anyway, what else...Oh, then there's the milk pooling on the mantle and the shattered glass it was in beforehand, and the broken Christmas cookies scattered about the hearth. And the pool of blood smeared down the hallway to just before the bedroom door. No weapon, though. Yet."

The chief went quiet, propping a leg now on the garage door, the thing giving up a groan under his weight. He took another drag before flicking the spent butt out into snow piled high at the edge of the driveway. It sizzled, sinking into the bank and leaving behind a black bullet hole.

I took a breath and folded my arms, dipping my head toward the driveway. "Sounds like quite the scene."

The man snorted a laugh. "You could say that. Add to that the fact no one inside ain't talking and, yeah, Merry Christmas to us, right? This tale writes itself, doesn't it?"

I furrowed my brow, not following.

He lit up another cigarette and seemed to notice, explaining, "Parent gets stabbed on Christmas morning. Kid caught in the middle of the fight. A whole pant's load of questions with zero answers. No one's talking."

I grunted. "Sounds like quite the tale."

"At least it's not a child-endangerment story."

"Child endangerment?" I asked, not understanding.

He took another drag of his cigarette and finished it, flicking it into the same pile of snow and throwing up the same hissing protest.

"Yeah, you know, some kid put at the mercy of some villain, for ransom or some other deranged reason."

I twisted up my brow. "On Christmas?"

He shrugged, rubbing his hands together at his mouth before blowing into them.

"What kind of crazy-ass nonsense do you read, anyway, chief?"

"Hey, I'm not the one who writes that crazy-ass nonsense!"

"I guess that's right."

He motioned toward the front door. "Come on, my nuts are about to freeze off. Gideon's inside sequestered with the suspects, not letting us talk with them yet. Clock is running out on that one, and I'll imagine he'll want you to look over our shoulders while we do the real work of putting the pieces to this godawful case."

I clenched my jaw and felt my nostrils flare involuntarily. *The real work of figuring out the case.* Heat ran up the back of my neck at that line the chief liked to throw around to put me in my place.

But I put on a grin, waving my arm toward the front door. "Lead the way."

The chief turned to go inside when I asked, "The ambulance, who was inside?"

He looked off down the country lane, not a car or sound to be heard now. "Go see for yourself."

I frowned. "Merry Christmas to us, is right?"

"You have no idea."

Chief Roller led the way down a cement walkway pockmarked by age and weather, a short set of stairs with a rusted, chipping steel railing leading to the door. An office on the way out opened it for us, and the chief held it open.

"Ladies first," the bald man said, a chipped front tooth winking at me through his grin.

Not taking the bate, I instead took in a fresh, cold breath and headed inside.

I'm glad I did.

Because it was hot as Hades inside the Robergs's house, a suffocating mass of humid air belching from deep within its bowels. Furnace had to be cranked to 80, it was so dang hot. Reminded me of Mother's house before she passed, God rest her soul.

But that wasn't the worst of it.

Riding high on that dragon breath of suffocating air was the breakfast leftovers from earlier that morning, the stench of cheese and bacon grease mixed with stale coffee and cinnamon and frosting washing over me, mixing with pine and laced with the tang of copper.

The tang of blood...

Almost bowled me over, it was so bad. How the blues could stand it was beyond me. Once I got over the heat and the stench, I was able to take in the lay of the land.

What I saw wasn't pretty.

Front door opened into the living room, a modest thing that stretched to the right with a short walk forward into a knotty-pine breakfast nook, kitchen stage right I figured. In that part of the house, chief roller was mingling with two uniformed blues and a detective in a Spartan sweatshirt and jeans huddled over a laptop. Sort of unprofessional, especially his support of Michigan State, but it was Christmas I supposed, and a man has to have his team.

Back my way, that copper tang showed itself in a smear stretching from stage left up a hallway I assumed led to the bedrooms ending in the Rorschach inkblot. Still didn't know who's that belonged to. But given that this wasn't a child endangerment tale, per the chief, had to be either an intruder—which I wasn't thinking likely at this point, since Gideon was huddled somewhere with the rest of the family—or a parent.

Which wasn't something I was ready to think about at this point.

Back to the living room. Place looked about what Chief Roller described.

A disaster zone.

A nice blue spruce had keeled over in the middle. Star popped clear off and lay a foot away, still blinking and attached to a string of those newfangled LED lights. Hated those things. Messed with my eyes something fierce. Why can't people leave the past well enough alone that you got to change up good ol' fashioned Christmas light bulbs? And I'm not even talking about the big ones Lynn and I had strung around our first Christmas tree back in the 70s.

Anyway, the tree was still decked out in those lights— red, green, blue—and a crap-ton of tinsel that reeked a bit of National Lampoon. But, hey, who am I to judge? You had the standard fare of ornaments: the basic Blue-Light special kind, round orbs of mass consumerism; the step above, your owls and snowflakes and Baby Jesuses; the elementary craft variety of misshapen glued popsicle sticks and sequined-covered pine cones. Most of them still clinging to the tree for dear life.

Then there were the others that had either flown the coop when the tree toppled or had been ripped off by someone on an anti-Christmas rampage. Fragments of crushed bulbs of all variety of colors littered carpet like confetti, along with those homemade craft ornaments torn to shreds, construction paper and paper plates and those popsicle stick peppering the same floor. Place was a mess.

I walked over to the tree a nearly stepped on the child-size Santa the chief mentioned. The decapitated head, too, a volleyball-size knogin with white stuffing blooming out like white blood from his neck. But no body. Creepy seeing the jolly giver of toys in that shape. Unnerving, really. Perhaps as unnerving as the cheesy eggs stuck to one wall with a splatter that was smeared down to the carpet below and milk curdling now on the mantle.

The rest of the floor was littered with torn wrapping paper and leftover Amazon boxes. A few toys were scattered about—Legos, Hot Wheels cars, a Barbie and American Girl doll—all of it adding up to the still life of Christmas morning.

I planted my hands on my hips and sighed, making a sweep of the room that was foreign to me. But for the few years I'd been married to my sweetheart, this sort of

Christmas was as foreign as the moon. Growing up, my family was the farthest thing from the *Leave It to Beaver* that was raised up as a model for middle-class American family life. It's why I went to Nam. Minute I turned eighteen, I marched down to the Army recruiting office and put my John Hancock on the enlistment contract's dotted line. Next week, I was off to basic, two weeks before Christmas, which was usually hell.

But this...the scene before me, on Christmas Day of all days. Head shakingly sad.

Couldn't help but notice a large portrait of the Robergs hanging above the couch on the far wall. A pastoral scene in one of those faux Victorian fake-gold frames. The smiling blond couple surrounded by equally smiling blond children, five of them, except for Timothy, their oldest, who had dark hair and brown eyes. An odd duckling, I supposed, his genes filtering down through someone's family tree somewhere. But they looked like your typical all-American, small-town Junction family.

Perfect teeth and smile, perfect hair and pose.

But I knew better. Thirty years in the priesthood taught me that. Ten years as a P.I. even more. And that wasn't even counting those eighteen years growing up.

Voices filtered from behind. Sounded like Gideon and his partner Lizzy, along with a child's. Boy, teenager.

Above that a whistle was thrown up from the kitchen table.

I turned toward the sound. It was the chief, the front of that eight-ball head of his wrinkled with annoyance and both hands of sausage fingers gesturing toward the hallway.

"Come on, Papadopoulos. We ain't got all day. Especially since it's Christmas!" Then he whistled at me like a dog again. "So hop to it and get Gideon squared away. We're ready to take him to booking."

Him...

I swallowed and nodded, quickly exiting stage left toward the voices down the darkened hall, minding my steps around the pool of blood shining like a crimson ice patch in the dim light and on past the smear that started in front of the far door at the end.

Knocking gently on the door, I pushed through it into a modest room, a dresser greeting me with Hot Wheels cars lined dutifully along the top, a pile of clothes thrown in the corner, along with a twin bed at the far end.

Sitting on it was the dark-haired kid, Timmy. Next to him was Kenny, as Swedish as they come from those Nordic countries, or wherever. But no Barbara, so good chance she was in the ambulance. Although, none of the other kids were around either, but I didn't want to go there. The chief said this wasn't a child-endangerment tale, so I focused on what it could be instead.

Even then, those possibilities were far from sugarplums dancing in my head.

Gideon looked over at me and nodded, waving me inside and Lizzy regarding me as well from next to Timothy. The defense attorney was white as a sugar cookie, face drawn and sporting a rival Michigan sweatshirt to the Spartan one on the detective at the dining room table. Supposed Christmas crises afforded a certain relaxed dress code, but now I was feeling overdressed in my blue gingham and dark denim.

Father looked worse, Kenny's face far from holly-jolly red. More cranberry, blood-red even, matching the streaks paving my way from the living room to the bedroom. Cheeks were wet, too, like melted snow under blood-shot eyes, an arm slung tightly around Timothy's shoulders.

And the son...well, for one his eyes hadn't blinked since I'd entered the room; didn't raise his head in acknowledgment, either. He wasn't wearing a shirt, and his black sweatpants were hanging low around his hips and bunched at his knees. Skinny arms held those knees up to his skin-and-bones rib cage that was heaving up and down like he was running a marathon. Most alarming were his arms and shins, bruised and bloodied.

Whether his or someone else's, it wasn't clear.

Not the way Christmas is supposed to be, that's for sure. No holly jolly for the Robergs this year.

Gesturing toward me, Gideon said quietly, "I believe you know Johnny Pope—well, Papadopoulos," he corrected himself, neither Kenny nor Timmy stirring. "He's one of my top investigators I hire for these sorts of..." he trailed off, face growing more ashen. He swallowed and met me at the door.

Back turned to the rest, he took a breath and said lowly, "Thanks for coming, on Christmas of all days."

"No problem." I glanced back at the bed, no one stirring. Then replied in the same tone, "Hate to say it, but please tell me this was a home invasion gone bad."

"Hate to say it, but wish it were that simple. Wouldn't have had to drag you out here, that's for sure."

"Where are the other kids?"

"Neighbor's house."

I nodded, regarding the remaining Robergs. "What do you know about what's happened here? Chief didn't tell me anything."

"What I know is that they're close to hauling in someone soon if nobody talks. He's doing the family a courtesy, seen as how it's Christmas and all. But the fuse is running short."

"Then you better give it to me, Gideon."

The man took a breath and rubbed his hands against his face, leaning in closer. "All I know, is there was an argument between Timmy and the parents about something neither of them are sharing. Someone got knifed, lots of blood spilled. And no one is saying a word—not even to me!"

"Just tell me none of the other kids were in that ambulance."

He shook his head, saying only, "Barbara."

I sighed and nodded. "Suppose that's a saving grace in this whole affair—whatever it is."

"The only saving grace given..." He trailed off, glancing behind and saying nothing more.

Which was not like Gideon. Usually never at a loss for words. Always in control of his emotions and in control of a crime scene, acting as an anchor for his clients. So seeing him like this was unnerving. What the heck happened?

There was a rapping at the door, snapping Gideon's head back to me and making me startle.

"Gideon, it's time," Chief Roller announced from the other side before cracking open the door.

A sob erupted from Kenny, the man throwing his other arm around his son, who sat stoic and unmoving.

Until he didn't.

Timmy stood, turning with outstretched arms, hands pressed together as if he were waiting for what came next.

Handcuffs.

A uniformed officer pushed past the chief and between Gideon and me, bearing those instruments of confinement as Kenny kept at it, the man growing louder and grasping for his boy while Lizzy tried her best to keep the dad calm.

Until he too stood and lunged in front of his son, yelling: "I did it! I'm guilty. Take me!" Hands were outstretched and pushed together as well—like son, like father.

Which instantly snapped Gideon into lawyer mode. "Say nothing, Kenny!" he yelled. "You either, Timmy." Then he turned his attention to Chief Roller: "This is clearly an excited utterance, said under duress!"

The chief snorted a laugh. "Duress? You've got to be kidding me. Take 'em both in." He waved down the hall, and another uniformed officer appeared, withdrawing another set of cuffs.

"No!" Kenny shouted, struggling now in the cinched cuffs under the one officer's handling. "He didn't do anything! It was me!"

The officer didn't like that too much, the burly man grabbing him by the arm and telling him to move.

"Shut up, Kenny!" Gideon shouted. "Not another word."

"But I—"

"Not another word!" he repeated before putting an arm around Timothy and instructing him, "Talk to no one, say nothing to no one, you got that?"

Kid didn't move, those unblinking eyes on that scrawny body staring forward.

"That goes for you, too," Gideon added, pointing to Chief Roller. "He's represented by counsel. They both are. Under no circumstances is he or Kenny to be questioned until I get there."

The chief put his hands up, that chipped tooth gleaming through parted lips. "Understood, counselor. Wouldn't dream of it. Not on Christmas, of all days."

The officer guided the boy out, Lizzy close behind.

"I'll be right there," Gideon said to Lizzy. "I need a minute with JP, but go to the station and don't let either of them talk. Especially Kenny!"

"Got it." She nodded and left, the father crying out again and Lizzy trying to shut him up.

Gideon mumbled a curse below his breath, waiting until everyone had cleared the hallway. Then he closed the door.

"What do you need from me?" I asked.

"Did you see the scene outside?"

"Sort of hard to miss."

"Anything?"

"You mean, did I find anything besides the toppled Christmas tree and decapitated Santa head? What the heck happened out there, Gideon, really?"

"I don't know," he said, raising his hands. "I'm telling you, neither one is talking."

"Then what do you *think* happened?"

He ran a shaking hand through his thick black hair. "Have no idea! You saw what happened. The kid...he stood, which tells me he did something."

"Or he's covering for what his dad did."

"Right. And then Kenny bolts to his feet to take the fall! So who the hell knows."

Ain't that the truth.

I rubbed my chin, ready to get to it. "I'll get to work and call you the minute I get a read on the situation."

Gideon put a finger at my chest. "The second! There has to be something out there we can use. Because none of this is adding up."

"Not sure the chief will be too keen on me poking through his crime scene."

"It's our crime scene too!"

I raised a brow. "Not really."

"Then go out and talk to the guy. See if you can get a sense of what they know. Just...do what you need to do, alright?" Then he stumbled back, his face falling and shoulders deflating again until he slumped on the bed, totally spent.

"I was Kenny's best man, you know. In their wedding, twenty years ago."

"No, I didn't know. Is—" I stopped short, catching my own breath, knowing there was another actor involved in this Shakespearean Christmas tragedy. "Is Barbara going to be alright?"

Gideon looked at me, shaking his head. "I don't know. She lost a lot of blood by the time I got there."

I took a step forward. "By the time you got there? When did you arrive—before the police?"

He leaned back on the bed, taking a beat for the words. "Kenny called me, his friend, when it all went down."

"So you got here, and then you were the one who called the police?"

He nodded, saying nothing.

"And what did you find?"

"What you found. The tree toppled over, ornaments smashed and presents scattered. Timmy locked in his room, hysterical and not coming out. Barbara on the floor —" his throat caught with emotion. He swallowed before adding: "losing blood…"

I rubbed my chin again, the day going from bad to something out of a Scorsese movie.

"You better get going," I finally said, opening the door. "Lizzy's good, but they're going to need the O'Donnell touch."

Gideon clenched his jaw and nodded, resolve suddenly returning. "You, too."

He walked over, planting a hand on my shoulder and fixing me with determined eyes. "Find out what happened. Please."

"It's why you called me. It's what I do."

He left without a word, hustling down the hall and out the front door.

Then I got to work.

First call was to my cousin Vinny—yep, true story. With a last name like Papadopoulos, there'd have to be a Vinny up the family tree. He's one of those fellas who has ways of getting things I can't. Like financial records and criminal records, civil judgments and birth records, property liens and other various-and-sundries scattered across the ether of people's lives. Digital and otherwise.

Vinny wasn't particularly thrilled with the timing of the ask, but I promised him I'd ship him some of my baklava. That did the trick. Said he'd phone back when he sent his bots across the internet to gather the goods, whatever that meant.

Next step was looking for answers. Starting with ground zero.

Timmy's bedroom.

Started with the drawers, because that's where the kiddos stash the good stuff. And stuff there was, mostly a few Maxim magazines stuffed beneath a pile of sweatshirts. Maybe Barbara found them and got into it with him? Who knew. More rummaging turned up nothing more than stale sticks of gum, a few more of those Hot Wheels lined up, and dirty socks. Same for the rest of the room, not much more than even more dirty socks.

So back into the hallway I went, sidestepping the blood and heading toward the living room. First things first: that Christmas tree.

Pulling out a handy pair of latex gloves, I slid them across my hands and stooped down to the carpet riddled with broken ornaments. Then I grabbed the tree and began heaving it upright.

"Whoa, whoa, whoa!" the chief shouted from the kitchen, waving both hands around. "Whatcha doing, Johnny?"

I ignored him. "Looking for answers, is what."

"Messing up my crime scene is what!"

I didn't care. I kept lifting anyway. Besides, I had gloves on, so I was covered.

Carpet was littered with dry pine needles and a slew of broken ornaments cracked open like eggs and shattered into confetti. Those rainbow LED lights were sagging from the trees' branches, along with a tinsel drooping like hot taffy.

Lying underneath was a sight to behold.

The rest of Santa.

Headless and more of that white stuffing blooming from a hole in his shoulders. he was holding a bell in one hand and a sack of toys over his shoulder, so he still had that going for him.

And right through the gut was a kitchen knife. A chef's, by the look of it, the sturdy steel jammed real good through the center of poor Saint Nick. Crimson streaking both the blade and the handle.

As well as a baby picture. Boy, by the look of it, with a full head of dark hair. In the corner was a faded yellow date. *December 25, 2007.* Thirteen years from the day.

I looked over at that painting again hanging above the couch of the Robergs, an idea percolating as I held the tree with one hand.

"Alright, JP. Party's over." A hand clasped my shoulder. It was the chief himself. "Time to pack it—" I imagined the man saw what I just saw. "That's evidence!"

I snorted a laugh. "No kidding. You want me to bag it for you, too, or do you think your guys can handle it?"

The man's eight-ball flashed an irritated shade of red, that chipped tooth nowhere to be found.

"Don't worry, I didn't touch it. Would you like me to pack it up now? Maybe drop the tree so you can—"

"No, no, no!" He put out a hand and motioned for one of the uniforms with the other. "Just...hold it while we bag it."

I nodded and did. The Spartan fan sauntered over with an evidence bag the size of a garbage bag. Decapitated Santa looked worse inside the foggy plastic, the picture of the baby stuck to his generous gut with that chef's knife going clear through to the black handle.

The detective hustled back to his kitchen table, and I looked at the chief. "Can I drop the tree now?"

He rolled his eyes and nodded, walking off without a word.

I set it down and my phone pinged with a voicemail notification.

I took it out and held it up, surprised it hadn't rung. Then I saw the weak bars, the signal going in and out. I frowned and walked to a window, finding some juice. Which I didn't need, because the message saved to my voicemail inbox. I played it, one end of my mouth curling upward.

"Jackpot..." I muttered before sending off a text to Gideon that I was coming over to the station now.

"What was that, JP?" the chief yelled my way. "Find something we should know about?"

Shoving the phone back inside my pocket, I said, "Nope. Nothing you should know about."

Then I pushed back outside into the crisp waning Christmas Day, the sun at a Midwest afternoon angling behind stringy clouds just above a horizon of barren trees —satisfied I was sure I knew what had happened.

Didn't take long before I was walking into the Mill Creek Police Station at the north end of Main Street, the dueling scents of Lysol and cigarettes still burned into the mid-60s brick walls throwing up their memories. A sergeant brought me back to see Gideon, who was crammed into a small interrogation room the size of my one-stall garage, those cigarette memories hanging heavy in that room along with piss-pour coffee rivaling the stuff my parish church used to brew.

Kenny was standing in a corner next to a long wall of mirrored glass, Timothy was seated at a metal table strapped to the floor, Gideon was seated across from him along with Lizzy.

No one else stirred but Gideon when I walked in, who stood with wide, expectant eyes. "Tell me you've got something good."

I licked my lips, searching for moisture at a sudden surge of adrenaline. They were looking to me to deliver the goods. Goods, I could deliver. But good goods was not necessarily on the menu.

"Well—" I started, the door closing behind me with a rattle. I walked farther in, next to Timothy, still ashen and stoic. "I've got something. Can't say it's good, though. Especially depending on how it all shook down."

Gideon shook his head with furrowed-brow annoyance. "I don't have time for riddles, JP! What the heck does that mean?"

"It means, I found something hiding underneath the Christmas tree that not even Mill Creek's finest had found yet." I paused, looking to Kenny to take notice; he didn't. "The rest of Santa. And stuck to him was a picture of a baby."

"A baby?" Lizzy exclaimed, her blue eyes going wide and blond curls bouncing with surprise.

"A *picture* of a baby. Thirteen years old. Today, in fact. Cute little thing with a head of dark hair. Just stuck right to our decapitated Saint Nick, with a chef's knife."

Gideon gawped for words but didn't find any. Kenny sighed from the corner, and he turned to him. "What is this, Kenny?"

He didn't answer.

So I did.

"I got a guy named Vinny."

"Vinny?" Gideon asked, a brow raised.

"A cousin."

Now he frowned, as if disbelieving. "Really?"

I shrugged. "I'm Greek. Of course I do. Anyway, he knows how to get things. And by things, I mean records. Financial, criminal, and—" I glanced at Kenny again. Nothing but a blank stare at the floor.

"And what?" Gideon asked with irritation.

"Birth records," Kenny said from the corner, head still down. "Along with adoption records, isn't that right?"

I nodded, Gideon cutting me off at the pass.

"Adoption?" he said before glancing down at Timmy.

Now the man pushed off from the wall, the strain in his face amplified by the fluorescent lighting above, made all the worse by the two-way mirror wall to his right. He was a man readying his confession. I could see it coming.

"We'd been trying to get pregnant for years," he started, "with no luck."

"How many?" I asked, figured I knew the answer to the question but wanting to hear it from him.

He blew out a lungful of air through pursed lips. "Five, six years. I'd blamed Barbara, like an idiot." He chuckled to himself, shaking his head.

Gideon glanced my way, face almost as pained as Kenny's.

"So one night," Kenny continued, "I blew off some steam."

"You blew off some steam?" Gideon asked. "What does that mean?"

Kenny didn't answer, not right away, but Gideon put it together. "An affair, you mean. Resulting in an unintended pregnancy."

Silence filled the room at the revelation. Then it didn't, the gentle sobs of Timmy filling the void.

Kenny cleared his throat, then continued, "When...well, his birth mother contacted me a few months later, I went straight to Barbara and confessed. Told her all about it. Didn't hide a thing."

"Right after you did," Gideon said with bitterness.

"I don't need your judgment, Gideon," Kenny shot back. "Six years we spent trying, alright! But then the Lord gave us this—this miracle!"

"Like the Virgin herself," I muttered under my breath.

"That's right," Kenny said, hearing me across the way. "You understand then!"

"Which is why you weren't on the adoption certificate." I said. "You were his biological father, which gave you legal rights to parenthood, but not Barbara."

"We agreed to pay for her to bring Timmy to term. She didn't want to go through with it, the pregnancy, but Barbara and I agreed to pay for everything. We stood alongside her for six months."

He paused, looking to Timmy, whose head was bobbing at his chest in fitful sobs.

"And then you got your Christmas miracle," I said. "December 25, 2007, Timmy was born. Only your name was on his birth certificate, because you were his biological father. Barbara was only added as a legal guardian after the fact, on the adoption paperwork Vinny scrounged up."

"That's right, Barbara adopted him—we are *both* his parents."

I took a step forward, going in for the kill. "But you never told Timothy, isn't that right?"

Kenny didn't say anything, his falling face his answer.

"And let me guess," I continued, "you decided on his thirteenth birthday to let him know his true Christmas-miracle story. But it didn't turn out like you thought."

Kenny's face was red, and his eyes were watering now. "He just got so angry. Like we had kept the biggest secret from him—"

"Because you *DID!!*" Timmy was on his feet now, roaring with a rage I didn't think the kid had in him. He pointed a finger now. "You stole my childhood from me! You stole my mother from me!"

"No, we gave you your childhood, son!" Kenny said, more pleading than anything.

"Why didn't you tell me? Why did you *keep* this from me? Keep my *real* mom from me *ALL THESE YEARS?!*"

Something in me broke at that line. I knew all too well the fact we don't always get the family we would have wanted. Timmy never had a chance to meet the mom who gave him birth. Now look at things. All of it was a damn shame.

Kenny went to him now, hesitant but wrapping his arms around the boy, the two embracing.

They stood like that for a good minute, the pair sobbing into each other at what had been held secret, at what had unfolded in that room.

There was a knock at the door, and the chief came in. He rapped two fingers against his wrist.

Gideon put up a hand. "Another minute. We're almost through."

Chief Roller took a breath then held up a finger. One finger. Signalling their time was up.

"Sorry to rush this," I said, "But before I arrived in the room, the chief let me know another fact about the case you should hear."

"What's that?"

"The forensic evidence." I took a breath, then spelled it out. "Blood was Barbara's obviously. On the floor and on the knife."

"Knife?" Gideon exclaimed, turning to Kenny.

"The one stuck through the picture into Santa. Prints on the handle belonged to Timmy."

"No, no!" Kenny shouted, grabbing Gideon by the arm. "He is *not* going down for this!"

"What happened then, Kenny?" Gideon shouted. "Now or never!"

He swallowed hard, then nodded. "There—there was a struggle. Like I said, Timmy went ballistic. Started throwing things, the gifts and a plate of eggs of all things against the wall. Then he went for a knife and that's when he..." Kenny trailed off, face falling and chest heaving with breath, as if reliving the nightmare and not believing he'd lived it.

Gideon encouraged, "Kenny..."

"Then, he sliced off Santa's head and took the picture we'd wrapped of him in a baby in a box and stuck it to Santa's body." He spit it out so fast it was like he was expunging himself of the memory, trying to rid himself of it.

"Then what happened to Barbara?" I asked.

"She screamed after the—the incident and went for the knife. I imagine she thought he would do something to himself, harm himself or something. There was a struggle, her hand getting sliced in the melee, and then it happened. So sudden, so quick."

"I stuck her..." Timmy said, distant and removed from reality.

"You stuck her?" I asked.

He looked toward my voice, but not exactly at me, eyes glazed over and head wobbly and mouth open as if searching for an answer.

"It was an accident," Kenny said. "Plain as day. And if I have to, I will go to my grave—the chair if I have to, and say it was me." He took a breath, whispering: "I'm the one who did it."

"But the prints," Gideon said. "There's no way it—"

"I'll say I wore gloves! I don't care, Gideon. Timmy's not going down for this. It was all my fault, don't you see? I'm the one that caused it all. I didn't want him to know, but it was Barbara who wanted to share the rest of his story. She was so excited. Thought it would be the perfect Christmas gift. And now look at it!" He was screaming now—which brought in the cavalry. "*LOOK AT US!*"

Chief Roller was back, along with two other uniformed officers. He ordered, "Take them both into custody."

"What?" Gideon exclaimed. "Don't you think that's a bit premature?"

"Not really."

"Why not?"

The chief waited a beat, one end of his mouth curling upward with what I thought was a bit too much pleasure. "Because now this is a homicide."

Time hung. And then it didn't, the room exploding into pandemonium between both Robergs, the father and son sobbing with grief and Gideon barking orders to not say a word.

And me just taking it all in, my stomach going watery at what had happened to that perfect family that Christmas Day.

Soon, Kenny and Timothy were being read their rights, and then they were ushered out to booking. Everything was custodial now, and the gears of justice would begin grinding toward whatever outcome suited Lady Justice's fancy, come what may.

An ache was needling the middle of my forehead, the full retched weight of the day catching up to me now.

"Now there's a Christmas no one expected…" I said to no one in particular.

Gideon put a hand on my shoulder and outstretched his hand. "Thanks. You did good, JP."

I hesitated, taking a breath, but took it. "Not sure I'd call this good. But I suppose you can use something in their defense."

"Merry Christmas to them, I guess."

"And us," I added. "On days like these and a *Day* like today, makes me glad the Christ Child showed up when he did, to rescue and repair this broken, busted mess of life."

"Spoken like a true priest-turned-private-investigator."

I grunted a nod and we both left.

Sun was setting fast now as I returned to my truck, darkness encroaching upon the waning Christmas Day. I drove the ten minutes home from off of Main Street to find a work crew removing those downed limbs that had started my morning off so rotten—and a street full of Christmas lights lighting my way home. Consumers Electric had pulled a Christmas miracle.

At least I had that going for me after the long day.

Parking my Ford in the one-stall garage, I sauntered back inside, my breath blooming behind me and that ache growing into a migraine that demanded a good bottle of Scotch. I poured myself two-fingers worth, neat, and settled into my well-worn corduroy armchair next to the fireplace of white ash, the Christmas tree still lit from the night before when the power gave, throwing up a peaceful vibe that set the night right.

Grabbing my Bible, I turned to the Gospel of Luke, chapter 2, continuing a Christmas-night tradition stretching back to the early years of my marriage.

It was not a holy night, but a silent night, all calm and bright, just me and the Apostle Luke and my Macallen 12.

Just the way I liked my Christmas.

CLASS ACTION ACTION

A note about this story: In 2021, I published my 10th action-adventure novel in my Order of Thaddeus thriller series, "Deadly Hope." Much of it is set in Mill Creek Junction, and a certain PI shows up at a crucial part of the mission. This story is his side of that part of the story. If you've read "Deadly Hope," then this will be a fun back-story to that moment. If not, you may want to hold off until you've read it, because there are some spoilers in this one. You've been warned! Either way, enjoy JP's action story.

"DARK ROAST FOR JOHNNY POPE!"

Guess that was me. Didn't even know what I'd ordered; didn't know the right protocol when I did. Don't make coffee like they used to, that's for sure. None of that commie-pinko crap for me. Double soy this, triple venti that. Dolled up with all that syrup and foam and whipped cream. Black, straight, and American-made.

My normal joint was a no go today. Filled to the brim with those out of towners that had been coming in from miles away the past week. Surprised Starbucks was avail-able, given all the newcomers. Guess they hadn't notice on their way down Main Street to the carnival north of town. The charismatic healing revival service, or what-ever it was. Had been going on a few days now, and what I'd heard coming from that thing made my Catholic heart long for the good ol' days.

As in pre-Protestant Reformation days. That Martin Luther character really messed things up, posting his list of grievances like he did on that church door. Not that I disagreed with the fella. But after the Church splintered into hundreds of upstart Christian sects, things had never been the same in Christianity.

Suppose I was sort of biased, being a former Catholic priest and all. And it wasn't so much the charismatic part I didn't like. My parish was part of the charismatic renewal movement within Roman Catholicism anyway. So I was down with the ecstatic utterances and full, well-rounded expressions of the Holy Spirit. Including heal-ings and revivals, music that wasn't stuck in pre-Vatican II days. Could preach like the best of those Evangelicals who'd mastered the charismatic arts, too, bringing it home when I needed to.

It was the freelance religion I couldn't stomach. The upstarts divorced from oversight and any sort of grounding in tradition. Especially the sort that pushed a pay-to-play spirituality. Where God's blessing was dependent on the size of one's monetary gift. Seemed to smack of the very thing that Luther character protested against, the indulgences that sought relief from the flames of eternal judgment in exchange for a sack of gold coins.

Irony of ironies!

But that fight was for another day. Only thing I was worried about was getting my cup of Joe and a *New York Times* to start the day off right.

"That's me," I said. The pimply faced kid who looked young enough to be my grandson pointing to the white cup with chicken scratching scrawled across it in black.

I nodded and retrieved my drink, asking, "Where are your newspapers?"

"Newspapers?" he asked, fiddling with some hippie-looking machine hissing like a banshee and throwing up gouts of steam. Like he didn't know what I was talking about.

I frowned. Kids these days. "Yeah, you know. Those nifty new gadgets made of paper. Long sheets of pressed wood pulp that magically showcase the latest news items of consequence. You know, trade disputes, regional wars, the price of oil, the latest government sex scandal."

"Isn't that what Twitter is for?"

I twisted my face up in confusion. Twitter?

"Here, JP, take mine. I've read all I can stomach."

I spun around to find Annabelle Kirkland clickety-clacking toward me in patent black leather stilettos and holding out the day's *New York Times*, looking good as always.

"Now there's a gal with class," I said with a grin, retrieving my dark roast. "And how's the Junction's finest prosecuting attorney doing this morning."

She smiled, handing over the goods. "*Assistant* prosecuting attorney."

"Give it time. In no time flat you'll be running the

joint."

"Especially if I keep whipping your boss at trial."

I chuckled. "Don't you know it. Been up against O'Donnell lately?"

"Just scored a jury verdict against Gideon. He looked pissed, so I'd watch out."

"Thanks for the advice. Keep that up and I'll be out of a job."

She left for her morning and sat with my newspaper and coffee at a corner table. Popped the top to my grande whatever, readying for my first morning sip and taking a whiff of the rising head of steam—

And winced.

"What the..."

Smelled like cardboard and gym socks! Where were the earth and spice tones like last time?

Chancing a sip, I recoiled and twisted up my face. As much in disgust as revulsion.

It tasted like cardboard and gym socks, too!

But Millie's on Main was a no go, and I needed coffee. So I went with what I had, throwing back a swig and going with it before diving into Page One.

Scanned the headlines and shook my head. Just like Nam, is what it all was. The way every sector of our society had handled the past year. From government to media, corporations to the expert class on everything from the economy to science to medicine to crime. It'd all gone to pot! No trust left in anything. And it was all their damn fault.

Opened her up to the gutter and took another swig of brew, the chalky burnt taste growing on me.

When the front door opened with a *thwap*, and in walked the man himself.

Gideon O'Donnell.

Fella strode inside a few feet and planted his hands on his hips, looking this way and that until he caught sight of me in the corner.

Just great.

"There you are!" He hustled over and slid into the other chair. "Where have you been? I've been looking all over for you."

I raised a brow over my newspaper, taking a swig of the brew and trying not to laugh it all over him. "Where've I been? You really have to ask?"

Gideon waved a dismissive hand. "Doesn't matter. Something's come up, and I need your help."

I adjusted my grip on the newspaper and threw back another swig. "Sorry. It's my day off."

"Not with that contingency fee I pay you."

I sighed, looking back over the top of the newspaper, Gideon throwing me those pearly whites. Man did have a point, and he was one to make it in court if it came to it.

So I folded the newspaper and tossed it to the table, then downed a mouthful of coffee that still tasted like a gym bag. Better brew at the Golden Arches!

"Let me have it."

He nodded, taking a breath as if readying to launch into an opening statement. "This one's the big one, Johnny."

"Big? How big?"

"Product liability big. Could go class action, given what else has been going down in the Junction."

Which meant lots of legwork and paperwork and gumshoeing. All of which was my specialty. My jam, even. I nodded for him to continue.

"You know the Hansens."

Sure did. A dear couple from my old parish who could never have children. Fostered twenty-three of their own instead. So the fact O'Donnell was dropping their name in a case that involved a couple I knew from the past, with their hearts of gold—I was all ears.

"What happened? And who did it?"

He looked over his shoulder, then out the window and around. Like one of those network TV shows from the 90s, where the guy in the know was paranoid about being overheard by some unseen power. Not like Gideon, that's for sure.

He whispered, "Paralysis and blindness."

I whistled, shaking my head. "And you think some corporation did it to them?"

"Definitely." Leaning in now, he added, "Comida."

"Aren't they a food processing factory north of the tracks?"

He shushed me and put out his hands, as if telling me to keep it down.

Now I was getting spooked.

"That's right," Gideon said. "There have been some strange goings-on over there, and I think it's connected."

I raised a brow, gulping back another swig. "Strange goings-on?"

He nodded. "That's right."

"Like what?"

"I've got a whistle blower that says a few months ago

the joint was purchased by a family from out of town."

I shrugged. "So what? Not much of anything in Mill Creek is owned by Junction folk. Besides, isn't Comida part of a multinational conglomeration?"

"Yeah—"

"So what's the smoking gun?"

Gideon looked over his shoulder and leaned in again. I took another swig, trying to hide a giddy grin. This was too cloak and dagger for me.

He said, "My guy says a few weeks ago a bunch of trucks started hauling in loads of an off-the-books ingredient."

I swallowed. "Off-the-books ingredient? What, like arsenic or something?"

"Something like that. It was around the time the place was bought out, and then there were changes to the ingredients of a whole host of food products."

"Let me guess. The Hansens frequented said food products?"

A grin played across his face, and he brought his hands up together. Started wringing them too, like a kid in a candy store. Like he saw dollar signs flashing before his eyes. "That's right. TV dinners. Every night."

"Geesh. You sure it wasn't the salt that did them in? Have you seen those things? Or maybe gave them a coronary, with all the trans fats and high fructose corn syrup?"

Gideon leaned back with a frown. "Don't judge, JP. Besides, no coincidence our client started getting sick after all this stuff started going down at Comida. And that's not even touching on the others."

"Others?"

"You haven't heard? About Mayor Goodall and Katrina from the Baptist church? Even Max Blade got hit, it's so bad!"

Now I sat up. "Max?"

"That's right. Deaf."

"And it's connected to Comida?"

"Not yet. But that's where you come in."

Another swig, another glance at my newspaper. "Do tell."

He took away the newspaper. I protested, but lost the match.

Nodding, I folded my arms, waiting for my orders.

"My guy can get you inside."

"Inside?" I asked, shaking my head in confusion.

"That's right. Inside Comida."

Took a beat, it not registering right away.

Until it did.

"You want me to B&E that joint for your case?"

He shushed me again, looking around. "No! Not break and enter. My guy can legit get you inside. But it's gotta be tonight."

"And do what?"

"Take a look around. There's a main office on the floor at the center of the compound. Get in, rifled through the files. Maybe crack into their computer network. Find anything that gets us our slam-dunk win."

"And that's admissible in court?"

He smiled. "Of course. Something that will steer us in the right direction that we can find ourselves on discovery."

I leaned back and grabbed my chin, the scruff growing prickly and my enthusiasm in this latest act growing in the same direction.

But, taking a breath and taking stock of the windfall I'd get, I nodded. And that was that.

Gideon left me instructions inside a manilla envelope he slipped me under my table. Which was weird. Real weird, even for O'Donnell. But at nightfall I showed up at his joint in the building adjoining the one I was in, just trying to enjoy my morning paper and cup of Joe. No rest for the weary, I guess.

After the sun slipped beneath the horizon, I met Gideon in the parking lot out back. Introduced me to a character named Guy. Apparently Guy really was his guy. No last name, just Guy, a squat man with thinning brown hair graying two decades too early.

Guy had been with Comida since high school and had worked up to dock manager. Said he could slip me in through a truck, the white semi that was parked on a side street jutting off Main. Sounded like a decent plan to me, so the rear door went up and in I climbed.

Before long we were trundling down Main Street to the north end of town beyond the tracks. Drive lasted fifteen minutes, and wasn't half bad. Truck bed had descent shocks and smelled like Grammy's cookies from childhood. The kind with sticks of butter—the real kind, not that hippie, New Age hydrogenated nonsense; and genuine vanilla—not that artificial crap they sell down at Meyer's General; and a few bags of chocolate chips that melted in your—

The semi slowed and a few voices interrupted my nostalgia.

Sounded friendly enough. Probably the night watch shift keeping track of the goods coming and going. For a split second I worried they'd open the hatch, but soon we were trundling back to it, the back end swinging around to a stop before the thing backed up into what I assumed was one of the bays.

Next thing I knew, the rear door was sliding up and Guy was ushering me out with a frantic hand-wave.

I complied, hustling out into a large monstrosity the size of my old high school basketball gym where I'd made the All State Finals 3-point shot that clinched our championship—back in the way-gone day. Smelled better at least, that memory of Granny's cookies flaring up again, along with a curious mix of gravy and potatoes, cheese and sauce, even grape juice and crackers, which was odd. Looked like the global conglomerate had diversified.

Joint looked like it extended quite aways, a mawing opening leading into another gymnasium-size room. All filled with steel vats this and steel conveyors that, all connected to steel boxes of varying sizes. If the price of steel shoots through the roof, I'll know where I can come swipe some to sell on the black market.

Guy motioned me over to an unpainted concrete wall

"Sam'll be passing around inside," he said. "Not all that stealthy, so you should be able to avoid him, but watch your six."

"Who's that, some guard dog or something?"

Guy snorted a laugh that echoed too loudly for my

taste. "Night guard. More like a poodle than a doberman, but he's got a radio and knows how to use it."

"Point taken."

"Last of the trucks left for the evening, along with the last shift, so you won't be bothered."

"Suppose I should get to it then before Poodles comes to make his rounds."

Before I left, Guy handed me a crowbar.

"What's this for?" I asked.

He shrugged. "Never know when one might come in handy."

I frowned, almost mentioning the Heckler & Koch stuffed at my back, but thought twice about it. Might have a change of heart if he knew he was secreting a P.I. packing heat inside his place of employ.

Instead, I grabbed the bar and thanked him, then off I went into the wild steel yonder.

Made quick work weaving through the maze of buildings connected by the jungle of steel conveyor belts running this way and that. Gideon had said there was a main office planted at the center of it all, confirmed by Guy. Soon enough, there it was.

I made for it, windows dirtier than my F 150s sitting square in the center of it all.

Hustling up to it fast, I stopped short at a noise.

No, not just a noise.

A humming, then a whistling before some tune being sung off-key.

Edging back around the main office area, I spotted it. Or him, rather.

The night guard Guy had warned about. Poodles.

About what you'd expect from them sort.

Short, squat, and hair thinning on top a bulbous head. Wore a dark polyester uniform that screamed Rent-a-Cop.

I stood still, just eyeballing the guy heading down into another room down aways. Thankfully plenty of air between me and him, but still I dared not breathe.

Decided to follow him. Make sure he wasn't going to be an issue, the crowbar in my hand reminding me of my options. As well as the H&K nestled at my back.

Padding along the concrete floor, the rubber soles of my shoes flaring up a squeak that made me think the owners were anal about waxing them suckers, I came up to the edge of a concrete wall looking into the next room. Same jungle of steel and maze of conveyor belts.

With one addition.

A door.

Shut, but promising. Because Rent-a-Cop was at it and pulling out a small packet of something from his rear pocket. Camels, from the look of it. The white stick sliding out and into his mouth confirmed it. Right before he pushed through into the night.

One end of my mouth curled upward. Couldn't help it. A cigarette meant a smoke break. Which meant I had time to get the job done. Especially with the only soul in sight no longer in range of whatever I cooked up.

The door shut with a clatter, but I held my ground. Leaned against the wall with a palm against the cool, smooth concrete, one eye trained around the corner while holding that crowbar fast. Took a beat to confirm it all, but silence enveloping the factory put my mind at ease.

Satisfied, I hustled back to the main office door. Grabbing the handle, I twisted it to open.

Locked.

Just my luck.

I gripped the crowbar in anger, peering through the grimy door window.

When I had an idea.

I looked at the thing in my hand and shrugged. Apparently Guy was right. Never knew when one might come in handy.

Glancing over my shoulder and waiting a beat for any sound, any movement, anything at all that would tell me the place was occupied somewhere.

Nothing but the sound of my breath. Not even no HVAC hum, which was surprising, but what did I know about running a multinational food processing conglomerate.

What I did know was how to break into a locked office.

With one swing of the crowbar, the handle sailed into the air and landed on the concrete with a clang.

Glanced around again but knew I was in the clear.

The door swung easily inside on hinges that hadn't seen an ounce of oil. The squawking was worse than the clang, but all that mattered was I was inside.

This joint had no style whatsoever, with scuffed, plain white walls lined by metal filing cabinets instead of wood bookshelves under dormant fluorescent lights. Although the Mr. Coffee in the corner, glass carafe caked black, certainly felt close to home. An ancient PC desktop computer lay asleep on a green metal desk from the same 80s era. Might be able to open up the device for a look under the hood, but that would take time. Time I didn't have.

Withdrawing a penlight, I flipped it on and stuck it between my teeth. Then started rummaging. Through folders and stacks of paper, opening drawers and peeking inside banker's boxes. Nothing stood out, and I was getting frustrated.

So I took a breath. Was pushing too hard, letting the clock set the pace. The time it took for Poodles to strike up a cigarette and continue on his rounds. Needed to be mindful, but needed my head in the game, too.

Closing my eyes, I took another breath.

When a noise startled me, sending me for the Heckler & Koch nestled at my back. In one motion, I whipped it out and spun toward the door.

There it was again. A slapping sound.

Like feet padding through a concrete monstrosity, steel this and that strewn about.

Crouched real low now, getting behind the desk butted up against the one wall perpendicular to the door.

I could hear them padding my way—swishy, squeaky scrambling sounds now along the floor as a pair of hostiles got closer.

Adjusting my grip, I chanced a glance, popping up above the pile of middle-management detritus.

And frowned, heat running up my back at what I saw heading my way.

There they were. Two of—no, three of them.

Great…

Nearly at the open door now. Had to think fast.

Which didn't take long.

Had something. Not ideal, but it might work.

Reaching into my pocket, I pulled out my phone. An upgrade from my dumb phone.

Flipping on the light, I swung it out from the void, the brilliant luminescence of my fancy iPhone blinding the lead hostile and sending him back on his heels. Not what I imagined when I bought the dang thing, but it worked. An added feature I should tell Apple to market.

"Don't move!" I commanded, growly and gravelly behind the brightness shielding the hostile from view. Put some real teeth into it, lighting up the perp with my phone light.

Young fella. About my height and half my age. Shaggy dark hair with a weapon raised that told me he meant business. A Beretta, if I saw it right. Not your usual civilian piece of firepower. Army-issued. Which meant this guy had military background. Maybe he was military.

This gig kept getting weirder and weirder.

Before I knew it, the perp echoed back to me the same command: "Don't move!"

Almost chuckled. Could tell the kid tried to sound convincing, with his Beretta back out in front. Wasn't working.

Another fella came into view. Bigger. Much bigger. Bald, too. With an Italian-made Sig Sauer that put this guy on the same level as Tweedle Dum.

"Yeah, pal. Not a muscle," Tweedle Dee said, backing up his man, but with the same squinting blindness.

My squinting brightness!

Two unknowns in the dead of night. Breaking into the same joint at the north end of Mill Creek that was at the center of some conspiracy poisoning my clients.

Not good…

Time to take back control of this god-forsaken night.

"I've got you in my sights, partner," I growled again, "and I ain't letting up. Now drop your weapons!"

The third guy complied, dropping to his knees. Not the others. Yet.

Tweedle Dum hesitated, the man with dark hair trying to get out from underneath my light but not able in the slightest. Could tell he knew they were sunk. Which did my little P.I. heart good.

I took a shuddering step forward, giving the light a shake for good measure—which offered the flash of a pistol barrel. My pistol barrel. Needed them to know I was armed and ready to fire, if need be. Not that I wanted it to come to that. But I'd get there, if need be.

"On your knees!" I commanded, tightening my grip and squeezing the trigger ever so slightly. Had to put her into gear, readying the beast if it came to it.

Tweedle Dum clenched his jaw and narrowed his eyes, throwing a glance over his shoulder to his partner. Tweedle Dum frowned but nodded him to comply. Knew the kid didn't want to. Not in the slightest. He glanced at the third man down on the floor, and his partner on his knees. Could see the wheels turning, trying to figure out the best way forward.

Which was down on the cold concrete with his pals.

Took a beat, then another, but the fella finally held

up his hands and joined them.

That's the spirit. Loosening my trigger finger back to resting position, I took a sighing breath of relief.

"Wait a minute..." a voice rose from behind the dark-haired fella.

Which sent my trigger finger back into activating mode and heart rate galloping back to full-on engagement.

Voice sounded familiar, too. Way too familiar. Almost like—

"Johnny Pope?"

Took a beat, but I instantly recognized the man. "Pastor Young?"

I swung my phone down to the third man on the floor. Didn't catch the fella at first. But—sure enough.

Peter Daniel Young. Same age as the other two, with dark slicked-back hair and dark clothes.

In the middle of my gig!

"Johnny Pope?" Tweedle Dee asked, the big fella with a bald head raising his hands and looking up at me in the light. "Sounds like a superhero."

"A Catholic priest, actually," Peter explained.

"*Former* Catholic priest," I corrected. "That was a long time ago."

"My bad. Sorry."

"Your last name's Pope?" the bald fella asked with a smirk. "Isn't that a bit too on the nose?"

I tightened my grip, irritation running through me now at the mouth on this one and confusion at the turn that had taken my gig down a sideways alley.

"Pope is my stage name," I explained. "Papadopoulos

is my last name."

"Ahh. Got it. Is that Dutch, or what?"

I frowned. "Greek."

"This is all very romantic," Tweedle Dum cut in, the military brat with more hair than I'd ever see again in my lifetime. "A meet-cute in a food processing plant, and all. Could make for an interesting bargain-bin romance novel, but would you mind sharing how the hell you two know each other?"

"And can we stand?" Tweedle Dee added. "My knees are barking something fierce!"

I motioned with my H&K before stuffing it at my back.

Beretta man stood, followed by his partner and the pastor. This had better be good.

"What's this about being a priest?" the man asked, the one with hair.

"Like I said, *ex*-priest," I said.

Peter explained, "He's a private investigator now, working freelance gigs."

"Which begs the question, Mr. Pope," he said, crossing his arms with interrogation.

I snorted a laugh. "Mr. Pope was my father. Johnny's just fine."

"Alright, then, Johnny. What are you investigating? Why are you creeping around in the dark in some food processing plant, breaking into offices and such?"

"I could ask you the same thing. Why don't we start with your names."

"We'll get to that, but seeing you here with these papers and folders all strewn about inside an office with a broken door and its knob lying in pieces on the floor—raises all sorts of questions."

I smirked, nodding toward the shattered knob. "That guy had a run-in with a crowbar."

Beretta Guy glanced at it lying on a table next to a stack of open folders. "Come on, man, give it to us. What's your business here?"

I went to answer but snapped my mouth shut, throwing a glance at Peter as if to ask if the coast was clear.

Peter nodded. "It's alright, JP. I imagine we're on the same side on this."

"Really? And what side is that? I don't even know who you are!"

"This here's Silas," Peter said, pointing to the man with the Beretta; sounded about right. "The other is Gapinski."

"We'll get to that as well," Silas said, putting out a staying hand and drilling Peter with a look that communicated clear irritation. Looked like this was his operation. I imagined the last thing he wanted was for it to get blown by some small-town P.I.

Couldn't blame him. I didn't want my operation being blown by some small-town pastor and his out-of-town lackeys. So we were on the same page with that one.

"You can trust them," Peter said. "They're with me."

I eyed Peter and the other two, putting all my stock in the reverend. Although, if you can't trust a pastor, who can you trust—even a Protestant one, and a Baptist one at that?

Taking a reluctant breath, I answered, "Gideon

O'Donnell hired me."

"Who's that?" Silas asked.

"Local attorney," Peter answered.

"To do what?"

I explained, "To provide some investigative background for a product liability lawsuit he's preparing to file against Comida."

"On what grounds?"

"On the grounds they made his clients paralyzed and blind!"

Silas didn't flinch at the revelation, throwing his man Gapinski a sideways look that was reciprocated.

Looked like they were in the know about something I needed to know about.

All in good time...

"Who are his clients?" Peter asked.

I shook my head. "Sorry. Can't say. Confidentiality and all."

"I understand that," Silas said, "but does this have anything to do with the carnival that rolled into town the last week?"

Now that was quite the bit of revelation-insight. Felt like it'd been dropped from on high. Like the Holy Ghost himself swooped in and handed me a word from the Almighty himself! Looked like we might be on the same team after all.

I took in a breath, crossing my arms now. "Why, is that why you're here?"

Was trying to regain control of my own operation, not wanting to let it get blown by some out-of-towners. Didn't think they'd take the bait, but it was worth a try.

"That's right," Silas said with a nod, the man giving a little—and probably wanting to get a little for it, too. "We're with the Order of Thaddeus. Gapinski and I."

I twisted up my face in confusion. "The Order of whatchamacallit?"

"When the carnival rolled into town a week ago," Peter explained, "I phoned a former professor friend of mine from the seminary I attended. Wanted to get his advice on what I'd seen. See if he knew anyone who could help us out. He connected me with Silas Grey, here, Order Master."

I chuckled, shaking my head. "Order Master? Sounds like some bargain-bin paperback conspiracy thriller."

"We get that a lot," said the man Gapinski.

"So who are you?" I asked.

"The good guys," Silas said.

I raised a brow at that, my blood boiling some at the presumption. "In my line of work, that's not always as clear cut as it seems."

Peter jumped in: "They basically defend the Christian faith from attacks, mostly from outside the Church."

"Like the Knights Templar, or something?"

Gapinski snorted a laugh. "No, silly! They ran from us down a darkened street in Rome!"

Silas sighed and shook his head. He said, "Look, we're here for the same reasons you are. To get answers. We've got good reasons to believe all the random illnesses affecting Mill Creek are connected to the equally crazy healings north of town at the revival service. And all the rabbit trails and loose ends lead here. To Comida."

That got my attention. "Really? Go on."

Surprisingly, he did. Explained his partner Gapinski had experienced some sort of paralysis, the same sudden onset neurological disorder that had affected others from the Junction. Then he really rocked my world when he said it seemed like the contents of the prepackaged communion cups being dolled out at the joint north of town had healed him—just like all the others at the revival service. He explained how the Lord's Supper was a central component to the sort of charismatic Word-of-Faith Christianity on display at the revival services. Yet he was sure however those Eucharistic elements 'healed' was less spiritual and more something else. Which he hoped to determine at the food processing plant.

I put a hand to my chin, disbelieving it all—and my luck. Two guys from some Navy SEALs for Jesus entity with the Church? Seemed too good to be true. And far-fetched.

But also seemed like a straight shooters who could be trusted. And given the fact this whole nonsense seemed like a conspiracy that spanned far beyond a couple from Mill Creek Junction, figured I could use all the help I could get. Also figured if they were with a religious order, even the militant variety, then we could work together.

"Sounds like we're on the same team after all." I stuck out my hand. "So why don't we get to it. We've got a lot of ground to cover if we want to crack the crazy."

Silas shook it. "So what have you found so far?"

"Not much. I'd only just gained entrance when you ran across my rummaging."

"What brought you here to begin with?"

Peter asked, "You said something about some product

liability lawsuit? What's that about?"

I nodded. "That's right. Gideon's client—well clients, a husband-wife pair, each suffered blindness and paralysis respectively. From what we can gather, it all happened after eating food made by Comida."

"Choco-Chocos," Gapinski said, "wouldn't happen to be on their menu, would they?"

"Not that I'm aware. Mostly TV dinners." Which I thought ironic now, knowing prepackaged Eucharistic elements were wrapped up in all the nonsense. Like Stouffer's dinners, those things were!

Silas said, "We best get to it." Looking to Gapinski, he added, "How about you and Peter have a look around the facility. Look for anything that we could use to link the contagion to the Bucks and the healings. Johnny and I will hang around here and sort through this paperwork mess."

Gapinski nodded. "Will do, chief." Peter looked reluctant, but he nodded as well.

The two left, then Silas and me got to work sorting through a mess of folders and papers in a cramped office that reminded me of my days in the priesthood.

Silas riffled through his file cabinet, the man huffing and sighing with clear frustration. Pulled out a folder and started shuffling through it.

"Find anything interested?" I asked, rifling through my own folder.

"Nothing but flour and corn syrup and any number of familiar gobbledygook ingredient names stuffed in most modern foods."

"I'll make up for your lack. Found something."

"What's that?"

"Shipping manifests."

Silas leaned over. "For what?"

"Acetylcholinesterase inhibitor, it reads."

"A classic chemical used in nerve agents, disrupting an enzyme that catalyzes the breakdown of acetylcholine, a neurotransmitter."

I looked at him with a raised brow.

"Something I picked up while working for the Army Rangers."

"Then maybe you also know what atropine is?"

"Sure. The antidote for nerve agents."

I nodded. Impressive. "Well, Comida sure ordered a helluva lot of both. Barrels of this stuff."

I passed the shipping manifest off to Silas. He scanned it with disbelieving eyes.

"Straight from a manufacturer in China," I went on as he read. "Came in on shipping containers bound originally for a shell corporation posing as a pharmaceutical company before making its way to Comida. Near as I can gather, it came disguised as a component of a muscle relaxing cholinesterase inhibitor."

"And with how inundated port inspectors are with these sorts of shipments, you gotta figure it passed easily without scrutiny."

Made sense to me. "And look at this." I held up another page and pointed to a scribble on a signature line that didn't ring familiar.

But seemed to spark something with the kid.

"Paulina Bucks?" Silas said with disbelief.

"From the charismatic carnival up the road?"

He nodded, lost in thought.

"Looks like your charismatic chickadee is running this joint."

"Looks that way…"

Gapinski appeared with Peter through the doorway, grinning from ear to ear.

"Find something?" Silas asked.

"You could say that!" He nodded to Peter. "Show him."

The pastor held up a clear plastic trash bag filled with chocolate cupcakes. Maybe those Choco-Chocos they'd mentioned earlier. Then he raised another, filled with the similarly familiar unleavened wafers.

Peter explained, "Found these next to conveyor belts way in the back."

"Just sitting there?" I asked. "Like they'd come off the same chute, right next to one another?"

"Exactly. Looks like someone forgot to take out the trash."

I snorted a laugh and shook my head. "Criminals…"

"What's better," Gapinski said, setting a jug of some clear liquid on the desk, "we found this junk farther back in a line running from vats that made their way into the final product."

Silas eyed it, throwing up a knowing grin.

"Sat in something labeled acolyteo—cholester—something or other. Couldn't remember how to pronounce it."

"What about acetylcholinesterase?" he said.

Gapinski's eyes went wide, and he looked to Peter in dumbfounded disbelief.

Peter nodded. "That sounds about right."

"How'd you know?"

Silas answered, "Because we found receipts of the stuff used to inhibit neurological function."

"Like causing people to become paralyzed?" Peter asked. "And blind or deaf, even?"

"Exactly."

"Always something..." Gapinski growled.

I folded the manifests I'd found and slid them inside my jacket. "So let me see if I got this right. Through their Comida operation, these Bucks characters are intentionally poisoning people."

"And then offering the only known antidote," Silas finished. "It's the only thing that makes sense!"

"That's messed up," Peter said.

"It's psychotic!" Gapinski growled, pounding a fist into his palm.

"Agreed," Silas said.

"But why?" Peter asked.

I shrugged. "Why do most people do anything with such brazen self-interest?"

"The Benjamins," Gapinski said with a nod.

"Money makes the world go round, my friend."

"And charismatic whack jobs bent on world domination."

"I don't know," Silas said, crossing his arms and widening his stance. "Seems too simple an explanation."

"The simplest usually is," I replied.

"You're talking about Occam's razor," Peter said.

"In my line of work, when a patient comes in with a cough and runny nose, it's safe to assume it's a head cold and not herpes."

"Eww," Gapinski said with a shudder.

"And in our line of work," Silas said, "when the Church is involved and there's a global conspiracy on the scale of the Bucks's operation that's undermining the historic Christian faith—things are far from simple, and there's usually a bigger player at work, or more."

Gapinski nodded knowingly. "Nous. Or that new Theoti outfit."

"Exactly."

I laughed. "Now you all do sound like some bargain-bin paperback conspiracy thriller! Which I don't even want to know about. Either way, we may not know the *why*, but we do know the *how*. Or at least have a pretty good sense of it."

Silas nodded. "Which makes this thing a whole different thing."

"How so?" Peter asked.

"We'd been assuming all the healings at the charismatic revival service were real. At least, I did, after I thought it was a load of nonsense."

"But they were," Gapinski said. "You admitted so yourself. Peter's friends, me for crying out loud!"

Silas shook his head. "No, not real. *Staged.* All of it. They fed people a poison that made them sick, across the world. Only to stage these healing events that offered the only cure. I don't know how this all works out, the technical science and medicine of it all, but that has to be the answer."

"I see what you're saying," I said. "It's like giving someone a cryptic note without the cypher. Could be a billion possibilities to unlocking the code."

"That's the way I see it, yes."

"And those prepackaged Eucharistic elements, the cup of juice with the little cracker slapped on top—they're the key, the cypher the body uses to unlock the cure."

"Exactly!"

"Then the delivery system for the original poisoning comes from this processing plant." I waved an arm toward the equipment outside the office. "From those damn TV dinners my clients ate."

Silas nodded "And the chips and snacks, the Choco-Chocos you ate, Gapinski."

"Always something..." he growled. "And there goes my appetite for junk food for the next decade."

Peter added, "Katrina was munching on a pack of the same snacks the day I saw the carnival the first time. Didn't catch that until now, the memory just surfacing. Then she got sick."

"There you go!" Silas said.

"But Torres didn't," Gapinski said. "I offered her one of my Choco-Chocos, but she didn't take one. Probably why she didn't get healed from the service, either. Didn't have the poison, or need the antidote."

Silas nodded with a frown.

Didn't know what they were talking about in the slightest, but it sounded personal. Like one of their own was sick, expecting a healing even, but was left high and dry. I'd counseled plenty of my share of such cases during my days with the Church. Those were the worst, the cases that were hopeless. Even more when they were looking to the Saints or Mary or Jesus to come through for them. Left me disillusioned a time or two. And given my own wife's death...I understood how they felt.

"From what I understand," I said, clearing my throat and blinking away a surprising rise of emotion, "Comida is a global conglomerate with facilities across the world, too. Not just localized to Mill Creek and the Midwest, or even the US."

"Let me guess," Silas replied, "they've got their fingers in places like North Africa and Brazil and India. The global hotspots for this blasted contagion that's been circling the world the past week."

"Sounds about right."

The group fell silent, all arguments and reasoning having been spent.

"Only problem is," Gapinski finally voiced, "how do we prove it?"

"Know any pharmaceutical scientists?" Peter asked.

"Or an epidemiologist?" I said.

Silas frowned. "I just hope Celeste and Torres can put the final pieces together..."

"Or the world is screwed," Gapinski said, shaking his head.

That was pretty much the long and short of it.

Silas went to answer when a sound caught his attention, then mine—and a glimpse of something caught both of our eyes.

Through the doorway, in the distance.

A door on rusting hinges, giving way to two men in black. Moving toward our position.

And fast.

Weirder and weirder...

No room to think about what came next. Had to act faster than the incoming hostiles.

Silas looked at me and Peter. "We've got two unknowns in black coming up fast."

I immediately withdrew my H&K.

"Put that away! We've got seconds to act, and that's going to do nothing more than scare whoever it is who's coming our way."

"What do you mean to do?"

Silas took a breath, then a beat. "You'll see. You two stay put. Don't do anything stupid."

Nodding to Gapinski, he gestured to the door and left without waiting for a protest from me.

A pair of heads peeking up above the parapet of food processing equipment were fast approaching now as the two modern Templars padded around a massive steel vat anchored to the concrete floor.

Just a few more beats...

And there they were. Right on cue.

The two hostiles rounded the office entrance, where me and the pastor were waiting.

As bait.

"Who are you?" one of them commanded in a Southern lilt.

"I was about to ask you the same," I said, voice calm, cool, and collected, betraying not a hint of what might come next.

Before I knew it, the two Order agents sprang from behind the hostiles.

Each taking one of the whack jobs with arms wrapping around their necks.

There was the expected struggle, but it didn't take long before both men were down on the concrete in no time flat.

"Check his neck," Silas ordered as he did the same to his own downed hostile.

Gapinski looked at him knowingly before leaning down for a look.

Pulling off the black hood, Silas yanked down the collar.

Nothing but white skin.

"What're you looking for?" I asked.

"A telltale sign of an old enemy."

His partner yanked down his hostile's collar. Then looked over at Silas and shook his head.

"What about the wrists?" Silas reached over to his own man as Gapinski did the same.

"What ancient enemy?" I probed, standing over them. "What're you talking about, and what aren't you saying?"

Silas looked at me, clearly hesitant to cough up answers. Reluctantly, as he searched his guy, he offered, "They're called Nous. An ancient enemy of the Church hell bent on destroying the faith. Terrorists who've been part of recent plots to undermine Christianity and bring about its destruction."

I turned to Peter. "Is this guy for real?"

Gapinski stood. "Clean."

"Same here," Silas said with disappointment. "Dang. I was sure it was Nous."

"Or Theoti, I suppose," Gapinski added.

"Who?" I asked.

"Just another run-of-the-mill terrorist whack job bent on destroying the Church."

"You both sound like that Dan Brown joker."

Silas ran a frustrated hand through his hair, ignoring my taunts. "If it's not Nous, or Theoti, then who the heck are these—"

A ricocheting explosion of gunfire overhead cut him off.

I immediately hit the concrete.

Just as the *rat-a-tat-tat* of automatic weapons flared up hot and heavy with relentless pursuit.

So Silas snagged the only option available to him, in a reversal of Michelle Obama's advice: When they go high, we go low!

He hit the deck and pinched off three *pop-pop-pop* rounds of this own, then again: *pop-pop-pop*.

Gapinski got the hint and joined the fun, adding his own *pop-pop-pop* to the mix.

Which the hostiles definitely didn't expect.

And resulted in their weapons suddenly discharging a *rat-a-tat-tat* rejoinder, spraying bullets out across the parapet of equipment and up the concrete walls to the ceiling.

Metal struck metal, this way and that—and something high above that wasn't any good.

Gas started hissing something fierce from a set of pipes at the ceiling, followed by the sparking of more bullets, the hostiles continuing their assault.

Which ignited the hissing gas into a flaming arc that reminded me of the flamethrowers in Nam.

"We better make a run for it," Silas said.

"Don't have to tell me twice!" Gapinski said.

"Where?" Peter hissed on a frightened breath. "How?"

"How?" I said with a smiling snort. "With your twinkle-toes feet, that's how. Come on!"

Without another word, I started off.

Silas grabbed Peter by the collar and shoved him after me, then pointed at Gapinski. "Go with them and make sure they make it out alive."

"What are you going to do?" the pastor asked.

"Make sure we're not followed."

"But—"

"That's an order. Now go!"

Without waiting, Silas darted between two conveyor belts, popping off a pair of *pop-pop* shots to draw the hostiles' fire and attention.

It worked.

Angry *rat-a-tat-tat*s chased him as he slipped into an adjoining room, the fire growing from behind and blazing orange lighting his way even as thick smoke started following his trail.

Triggering a blaring alarm and the sprinklers from above!

Had to hand it to the fella. Guy had balls running into the fray of things like that. The fire fray of things!

But orders were orders. And no way in hell was I going to let Pastor Young die under these conditions. Even if he was a Baptist preacher.

I grabbed his collar and dragged him my way. "Come on, pastor. Now's not the time for heroics."

He went, but protested. "It sounds like Silas needs

us! Sounds—" the man gulped down air as much as the words he didn't want to say. "Sounds dangerous. They could be hurt. They could be…"

Pastorman trailed off, not able to voice the truth of the matter.

I let go, Peter nearly slumping into me.

Noticed the other guy Gapinski trailing behind and not at all caring about keeping up.

I spun the pastor around and said, "Look, kid, the guy clearly can take care of himself. If he's the Navy SEALs for Jesus like you make him and his partner out to be, they'll be fine."

Peter took a breath but nodded, the place filling with acrid smoke and dancing orange flames at the one end.

All of it quickly making its way toward us!

I grabbed his collar again, glancing over his shoulder at the seventh circle of hell coming our way!

And not seeing Gapinski anywhere in sight. Must have gone back for his partner. I would have.

Peter followed my gaze. "Where's Gapinski?"

"Probably to fetch his partner."

He went to go, but I yanked him back around.

"Not my job, and not my worry!" I yelled. "But you are, so let's go!"

He hesitated, turning back toward his friends somewhere in the hellish maw racing our way.

"Come on, kid. We've gotta get to it!"

Turning back, he nodded. Then we took off.

Not having a clue where we were going. Not in the slightest!

There was confusion all around. Between the

jumbled mess of conveyor belts going this way and that, a gauntlet of steel that gave no sense of direction, compounded by the billowing black smoke and fingering flames inching our way at the ceiling—I couldn't make sense of it.

Then Peter grabbed my arm. "Do you feel that?"

"Feel what, kid? The heat?"

"No! The opposite. A cool breeze!"

I did, but it didn't compute. "I don't…"

"We left the back door propped when we slipped inside."

I raised a brow. "You mean when you broke in and entered?"

He rolled his eyes. "Whatever. How did you get inside, anyhow?"

"I had help. Legit help."

"Didn't look so legit what you were doing when we came up on you!"

Pastorman had a point. And the breeze felt right. Like a trail of breadcrumbs leading us out.

"I like your idea, Peter. Let's get to it and adjudicate which of us was less of a lawbreaker than the other until after we escape with our lives."

Peter was right. A cool breeze sliced through the cloying heat and acrid smoke. Like the hand of God himself reaching through the gauntlet of equipment and rooms. Soon I caught sight of a door standing open at the far end of one concrete room filled to the brim with steel vats and belts and ovens. A window of stars silhouetted against the mawing darkness inside that was quickly turning orange.

"Come on!" I shouted, taking off toward the light at the end of the tunnel.

We reached the door in no time flat, the two of us gulping for air that smiled of pine and fresh-cut grass, cigarette smoke even.

Heaving a breath, cursing my age for not being as young as I used to be, I glanced down and saw someone leaning against the side wall. Looked like a guard.

"He ain't dead, is he?" I asked, motioning toward the figure who looked like the guard I had seen slip outside earlier.

Peter startled and followed my nod. "Goodness, no! We—well, Silas took him out at the start. Was our only way in."

I smirked. "Hmm-mmm. That's what they all say."

"Hey, I didn't know—"

Livid *pop-pop-pop* shots cut him off, followed by a crash from behind.

Jolted us back toward the inside, that's for sure! Our heads snapped back to the joint filled with steel conveyor belts and vats and concrete walls consumed by a phantasmic show of fire and fury.

Nearly left then and there, the heat of it all getting to me more than the smoke, which was just starting to billow our way.

But then I saw them. Silas and his eight-ball lackey. Running toward us overtime and double-time. Kicking up his legs and working his arms, like he was back in his teenage quarterback glory days or something.

"Come on!" Peter yelled, motioning toward the open door. "It's going up in flames!"

I threw the kid a sideways glance. As if I didn't already know with the fires of hell blazing all around!

But I knew it was the pastor's first rodeo, so I didn't say anything snarky. Soon we were all out into the darkened night, and I was gulping merciful lungfuls of air as much as the other fellas.

Peter and I took off for the fence, us two motioning for the others to kick it into high gear back to an opening Gapinski had apparently cut earlier. Didn't take long before the other two joined us.

"Thought you two were goners," I said, shoving Peter through the slit in the fence. Gapinski was next, then Silas, but not before guiding me through.

First man in, last man out. I got it after a tour in Nam.

Shoving through himself, Silas said, "Thanks for the vote of confi—"

BOOOM!!!

A phantasmic show of fire and fury from behind cut him off.

The force of the explosion tossed me like a rag doll. A punch to the back that sent me sailing, with head whipped back and arms outstretched as if coming in for an embrace.

The others went with me, by the look of it.

Took all of three seconds before I was eating grass and dirt, a fireball from Satan's abyss blooming behind with a scorching heat.

Turning on my backside, I took in the view.

The entire Comida complex was ablaze now, the night filling with acrid smoke billowing high and carrying along on a cool breeze coming in from Lake Michigan fifty miles due west. Wouldn't take long before the county mounties and their entourage of fire brigades from three counties over came riding in to save the day.

I stood, as did Peter and Silas and his pal. "Boy, I tell ya. You sure know how to show an old fart like me a good time."

Silas frowned. "Not what I had in mind."

I shrugged. "You win some; you lose some."

"Got that right."

He stuck out his hand; I took it.

"Thanks," I said.

"Thanks? I should be thanking you. Because of your help we found what we came for."

"Yeah? And what's that?"

Silas paused, looking back at the blaze. "Answers."

He didn't say anything more; didn't need to. Pretty well spelled it out for the both of us.

"Yeah, well," I replied, "thanks to you, we'll nail these knuckleheads in court. Class-action style."

"Hope so. But if we don't get out of Dodge, none of us will see this thing through."

Silas nodded to his partner and Peter, the three of them saying their goodbyes and heading off.

I watched the blaze from a berm lined by pine trees, sirens in the distance growing louder—and closer.

Took a beat to watch it all burn, sending up a prayer of thanksgiving for the roundabout way the Lord gave me a win. A secret religious order, probably housed in the Vatican no less!

Go figure.

CLOSE ENCOUNTERS OF THE JAE KIND

THE PLACE SMELLED of wet wood and those hippie-roasted coffee beans from that corporate joint downstairs. Last cup of Joe I'll ever get from that place, I tell you that! Tastes of cardboard and burned socks, it was so bad! Although it didn't smell half bad trudging up to the second floor of the law offices of Gideon, Winslow, and Seward.

My client. Boss, really, given the dynamics.

Still, the musty smell of mildew was getting to me, each step up the rickety stairwell of hardwood flaring up a new bout—probably of mold spores it was so bad. Could use an industrial-grade dehumidifier. Or maybe there was a leak somewhere. It'd been raining cats and kittens the last week nonstop, so that was a definite possibility.

Farmers on the westside of Mill Creek Junction weren't complaining, that's for sure! Neither were the celery and onions and cabbages, the beans and tomatoes and every other veggie under the sun that had put the

Junction on the map back in the day after the place was cleared of trees then milled and sent packing on trains that ran through town.

Reaching the top, I chuckled to myself and shook my head. Back in the day, when I was a teenage ankle-bitter, I'd hitched a ride on a westbound train headed to Chicago. The line ran from Detroit clear through Mill Creek Junction, picking up produce and other factory odds and ends by that time after the timber dried up. Had watched the thing hoot and holler on by after school almost every day for a decade.

Old Man whopped me good, he did. And good for him, because I was a terror! Would have kept at my terrorising, too, had it not been for the draft, and Nam, and all that had happened when I got back. But that's a whole other ball of ugly for another day.

My smile faded, the memory making me wish I'd made it to Chicago.

Hoofing it to the top, I yanked out my handkerchief and wiped my sweaty brow. Was sweltering on top of the stickiness, the dead-of-August heat pressing in like crazy and thickened by midnight storms that had been flaring up all week. Didn't Gideon's joint spring for air conditioning? Jeez Louise!

At least the hallway smelled of coffee. Not the tin-can kind, mind you, but the coffee shop variety, the vents from Starbucks next door working about as well as they usually did, but probably compounded by the heat. Stuffing the hankey at my back pocket, I turned my nose up and kept walking, much more preferring the tin-can variety, thank you very much!

Down the hallway was O'Donnell and Associates, so I picked up my pace as I was late as it was.

Door was one of those throwbacks. Gold ink set inside thick black edges in a sort of old-school banker-like serif typeface that harkened back to Mill Creek Junction's early days, the text set against frosted glass and arched with just the right amount of curve, a judges gavel set underneath in a sort of exclamation point that emphasized the justice they offered their clients. That we all did, my own investigative chops responsible for no small amount of victories.

If I played it right, the same would be true today. Whatever it was.

Reaching the door, I grasped the burnished bronze knob sweating as many buckets as I was from the humidity.

And stopped short.

Did my ears deceive me?

Through the glass door I heard, "Jae McCray to see Gideon O'Donnell."

My heart nearly stopped at the sound, and breath caught in my chest.

"Jay, you say?" a man said. Sounded like Reggie Winslow, one of Gideon's associates who was like him but half his age: black guy with an eight-ball head. Well, the eight-ball head part, not black guy part.

With a last name like Papadopoulos, I was Greek all the way. Son of immigrants who fled post-war Europe, more like it.

"That's right. With an E," Jae sounded with muffled intent through the door.

"For Gideon, our chief counsel?" another voice popped up, a woman. That'd be Lizzy Seward, a perky blond with a nice pair of legs.

There was a shuffle and a bit of mumbly mutters. Could nearly hear the gears turning from this end of things, knowing what the pair were thinking.

Then I heard: "Gideon's running late," Reggie said. "He'll see you in a few. Feel free to make yourself at home. Would you like a drink?"

And that's when I stepped in, the knob slipping from perspiration—its, not mine—but getting there eventually and pushing through.

I opened the door into the larger space of carpet the shade of mint Listerine from another century ago, walls white and blank and begging for some love with two dented wooden desks shedding their stain from some-time last century where Reggie and Lizzy slaved away for far less than what I made, which wasn't saying much.

And there she was. The itty-bitty firecracker who I had tried to help those many years ago. A hundred pounds wet with shiny ginger hair, long and layered and lying down her back. Had on cowboy boots and was wearing a duster. Like one of those vigilantes straight out of an old Western. Looked like she was taking her new gig out in Nevada seriously.

O'Donnell said he'd brought on some help. Last person I'd expected to see in these parts was Jae McCray, that's for sure. Especially with how we left things, and she left town.

The associates looked at me first, nodding their

acknowledgement to the other man invited to the mid-afternoon party.

Then Jae followed their gaze. And grinned, eyes brightening and mouth curling into a wide grin.

Not what I expected after we left things last, but I'd take it.

She folded her arms and kicked one foot behind the other, pressing the toe of her boot against the green carpet. "Jonathan Papadopoulos. As I live and breath."

Reggie and Lizzy threw each other a glance, them both mouthing *Jonathan Papadopoulos* in unison.

I frowned, then brightened. "Nice to see you again, Jae."

"Wait, you two know each other?" Lizzy asked.

"You could say that..." Jae said with a wink.

"Oh, you know we'll have to get the 411 on that soap opera later!" Reggie came out from his desk. "Can I fix you a drink?" he offered Jae.

I scoffed. "Hey, what am I, chopped liver?"

He laughed. "I already know your poison."

Now Jae laughed. "Don't we all..." She put a hand on my forearm, like I remembered. "But alas, just a Shirley Temple for me."

Reggie looked to me, then to her. "Alright then."

"Not only because I'm an old-fashioned kind of gal at heart, though not even cresting forty. But also because alcohol and me don't mix well. Last time it did was 3,691 days ago. Got my chips to prove it."

"Good for you," Lizzy said with a smile, pushing a strand of those blond locks behind an ear.

"Remembered it like it was yesterday," Jae continued

while Reggie prepped our drinks at the office minibar. "The day I found my lyin', cheatin', no-good sonofagun fiance with my maid of honor the night before our wedding."

"Oh, no!"

I cringed inside, the memory of what came next.

But she didn't go there.

Jae nodded at Lizzy. "That's right. By now, we'da had two-point-five kids, a two-story brick house perched behind a white picket fence. Cadillac on one side of the garage; Ford 150 on the other side."

She turned to me and smiled. "My side, of course."

Of course...

"But it wasn't meant to be. And after that, Grey Goose and me were like the British and Irish: never the twain shall meet. Yet, I insisted. And persisted. Leading to an assault charge that was later dropped. Against me, not to me; dropped by him for me."

Reggie walked up, eying the Shirley before turning it over, as if thinking twice about giving her even a non-alcoholic drink.

But she took it with a smile. "Thanks!" Then promptly took a sip.

I threw back a mouthful of my neat scotch. It was gonna be a long afternoon.

"Supposed I should have been grateful," Jae went on, "but that night was the final word on the ellipses of my life that had begun years earlier."

Reggie and Lizzy glanced at one another with wide eyes before they fell to the floor.

Jae laughed and put a hand to her mouth. "I'm doing it again aren't I. Oversharing."

Reggie said, "Maybe. Just a tad."

The door to the practice opened with a clatter and in walked the man himself.

Gideon said, "Mr. McCray, I'm terribly—"

Jae spun around next to me and folded her arms. I just stood there, trying to suppress my grin. Because I knew what came next.

O'Donnell stopped mid-sentence, a fit middle-age man wearing a blue suit in who was now mid-stride, holding his black leather briefcase in one hand and some Starbucks frufru drink in the other.

Jae turned to me. "Sorta cute, but a bit too old for my taste. Although, if I had daddy issues or was a decade older it could work. Or both."

He stiffened, then chuckled, dipping his head before scratching the back of it blooming red with embarrassment I could see from here like a neon sign.

"Uh, Jay McCray?"

"Jae with an E," Lizzy and Reggie said together.

Gideon's face flushed a more radioactive shade of red, which amused me. "Sorry about that. Didn't realize Jay was a "

"Woman?" I said, one end of my mouth curling upward now. Couldn't help it.

He frowned and shut the door before hustling our way.

"Gideon O'Donnell, by the way." Oddly, he waved instead of extending his hand in a greeting.

Which she offered instead.

He took a breath and threw me a glance. I shrugged and nodded her way.

He frowned again and shook it before taking off again. "Office is this way, if you don't mind JP and Jae."

Jae glanced at me, and I shrugged. "Suppose that's our gig walking away."

"Suppose so," she said.

"Didn't know you were working this one."

"Didn't know you were either."

"We good?"

She chuckled. "After the last gig you threw my way. You bet."

"How'd that turn out, by the way? Cave Creek, Nevada, right?"

Jae nodded, then leaned in. "I could tell ya, but then I'd have to kill ya."

Now I chuckled. "Fair enough."

"Time is of the essence!" Gideon shouted from his office.

"Suppose we better get to it," I said.

"Suppose so."

I led the way, followed by Jae and the other two attorneys. Apparently this one was an all hands on deck sort of case. Great.

Gideon's office was really just two walls slapped together to separate the main area from his own humble work abode, with two windows looking out into the main area. He was sitting behind a desk piled high with manilla folders spilling bent and misshapen papers. The room was darkened by pulled blinds, too, shading a century-ago wood desk bowing under the weight of too much work, a laptop anchoring a corner from back in college and a few thick cloth-over-board books fraying at the edges, the heat hovering with the same menacing molestation as the hallway and the outer room, but with far more ill intent. It was as if the hot humid air was clawing its way into my mouth and esophagus and lungs, it was so bad.

"Oowee it's hot as Hades in here!" Jae said, saying what we all wanted to say. "Forget to pay the electric bill?"

"One time," Lizzy said with a smirk, coming from behind.

"Air conditioner is fritzy," Gideon said.

"Again..."

"Yeah, yeah, yeah. Have a seat."

He motioned to two brown leather chairs that looked like Goodwill specials. Jae took one, I took the other.

"Sorry about earlier, Ms. McCray," Gideon said with a chuckle before taking a long swig of his frufru drink. "Sort of expected a—well, a man."

Surprised there was room in that yapper of his for both the sugary Starbucks nonsense and his foot.

A closed-mouth smile played across Jae's face. "I get that a lot. And Jae is fine."

"Never heard of a gal named Jay."

"Get that a lot too." Then she corrected, "By the way, that's Jay with an E. *Jae*."

He cocked his head to one side. "That your real name, or some sort of superhero name?"

"Do I need one?"

"Depends on your line of work."

"Suppose." Jae took a breath and girded for more. "It's a nickname. Short for Jael."

I suppressed a grin. Here we go...

"Jaw...eel?" Gideon asked.

"No, no, no," she corrected. "*Jael.* Jay. El. Like the letters."

Face looked like he'd swallowed a lemon turned inside out at the mention of it. "What the heck is that?"

"It's biblical."

Even more face twisting. "Biblical?"

"Yeah, as in, from the Bible."

Now Gideon leaned back, his chair throwing up a creak, and crossed his arms. I could see the wheels turning.

She smirked, readying to offer what he was thinking. "My father named me. He's a minister. Or, was..."

"Father, huh? And a minister?"

Jae nodded, saying nothing more.

"He passed or something?"

"Or something."

More turning wheels, but Gideon left it alone, instead going with: "Well, what kind of name is it, anyhow?"

"Jewish."

He raised a brow at that one. "Jewish?"

Jae raised a brow of her own. "And what kind of name is *Gideon O'Donnell*, anyhow? Sounds like a Jewish leprechaun."

He chuckled at that. "What difference does it make? It's the kind that's on your paycheck. Should you get one from this fine establishment."

She settled into her chair. "Fair enough."

I liked seeing this back and forth. Reminded me about the first time I'd met the firecracker myself a decade ago. After things went to hell with her engagement. And I was still a priest.

Back in the day…

Gideon took another sip of his frufru drink and asked, "You Jewish. Not that there's anything wrong with that."

Jae raised a brow. "With a name like McCray?"

He considered that. "Suppose that's the truth of it. You Catholic?"

Now I cleared my throat and crossed my arms, frowning for fun.

"Not that there's anything wrong with that, either, *Father*," he said with a grin.

"Former Father."

"Yeah, yeah, yeah. So what's it mean, anyhow? Jael?"

"You ask a lot of questions."

Gideon shrugged. "It's my job. Though Dusty did put in a good word for you."

She seemed to brighten at the mention of her new boss. Which was interesting.

"Apparently you either screwed off in Sunday School," she said, "or were never brought up in the Church to begin with."

Gideon smiled at that. "Apparently." He pointed at me. "And nothing from the peanut gallery."

"My lips are sealed," I said.

"Well, if you must know," Jae went on, "a prophetess of the ancient Hebrew people she sent her military commander to mobilize some tribes to do battle against King Jabin of Canaan."

Story was familiar enough. Not only because I'm sure I preached a homilie on the passage once, though wouldn't have known why, given the gory details. But also because she'd given me the same spiel.

"Uh, alright…"

"The fella didn't want to go unless Deborah, the prophetess, also went. But she advised that a woman would take the honor of the battle, not Barak her commander."

Now Gideon crossed his arms. "Uh, alright…"

"The head of Jabin's army was led by Sisera. One thing led to another, and before he knew it, the military commander was sleeping in Jael's tent."

Now he furrowed his brow. "And?"

Jae shrugged. "And my namesake took a wooden mallet and drove a tent peg through the fella's temple, nailing it into the ground while he was sleeping, killing him instantly."

Gideon loosened his arms and his face widened into a grin. "Sounds like my kind of gal."

"She might be. If the price is right."

Now he chuckled. "Sorry I asked. But with a name like that and a story to boot, glad you're on my team. And happy to have you on the team."

Jae startled, glancing at me with one end of her mouth rising with suspicion.

I shrugged, looking to Gideon.

"Just like that?" she said.

"Just like that. Dusty put in a good word for you.

Told me I'd be a fool not to hire you on. Didn't tell me you were a she. Not that there's anything wrong with that. But still. Would've been nice not to have stuck my foot in my mouth right out of the gate."

Her cheeks flushed, and she put a stray lock of hair behind her ear. Telling me there was more going on there with Mr. Osbourne than meets the eye.

"Why didn't you ask my old boss," Jae said, turning to me.

Gideon paused a beat, his brow furrowing as his eyes fluttered between us.

"You mean JP, here?" Lizzy asked, clearly as surprised.

"Didn't know you were an item," Gideon said.

I chucked, shifting uncomfortably. "Not an item. A team. Back in the day, and only briefly. A blast from the past."

"After he was defrocked," Jae added.

"I was not defrocked!" I said. "I left the priesthood on my own accord, thank you very much."

Now she shifted. "That's true. To some extent..." she added with a mutter.

Those eyes of Gideon's shifted between us again before he pursed his lips together and he shook his head.

"At any rate, how about we get to the reason for our little pow-wow."

"Let's," I said.

"Yeah, why don't we," Jae added, shifting a leg over her other and staring forward.

I admired her profile, that sloping nose and those chestnut eyes, complementing that ginger hair of hers that was still as perfect as the last time we'd been together.

And by been together, I don't mean *been together*. But seen one another, the day I helped her back to her feet after decking that loser fiance of hers.

A loud *slurp* from Gideon brought me back to the moment, the man eyeing me over the lid of his white Starbucks cup, black name smudged down the side.

"Now that we've gotten to know each other..." I said, shifting in my seat. "How about we get to the gig. Let's have it."

He swallowed and took a breath, scooting to the edge of his big wooden desk and pulling out a file. He handed it over.

I took it. "What's this?"

Taking a beat, and a glance at Lizzy, she answered, "Crop circles."

Those two words seemed to hang in the room, their three syllables sucking all sense of things from the space and leaving it with dumbfounded silence.

"Come again," I finally said.

Gideon shrugged. "You heard her. And heard her right."

"Crop circles." Took everything in me to keep from laughing the man out of the room. A snicker slipped through a grin. Setting the folder back on the desk, I said, "As in flying saucers and little green men?"

Now he frowned. "Yes, JP. Flying saucers and little green men."

"Are you serious?"

"Well, not the saucers and aliens part," Lizzy said. "You know Herb Warner, right?"

"Yeah. Man only owns the largest industrial farming operation in the Great Lakes."

"Right. Well, a few days ago, crop circles appeared in his cornfield on the south edge of town."

"And what does he want me to do about it?"

I said that part with a bit too much bite, throwing my hands up in exasperation at the silliness of it all.

Gideon leaned forward, putting his elbows on the desk and making his hands into a tent. Like he always does when he's getting into position to strike.

"Investigate," was all he answered.

"But why me? Why not Chief Roller with Mill ' Creek PD?"

"And why me?" Jae asked, leaning back with folded arms.

Gideon threw me a look that said shut it and get on board, right before he turned to Jae with a shrug. "From what Dusty said, you have some experience in that area."

She laughed. "Not crop circles! Crazy-ass weird, maybe, given what's been going down in Cave Creek…" Trailing off and shifting in her seat, Jae pushed her hair behind her ear, as if she revealed something she shouldn't have.

"At any rate," Gideon went on, "our client would like to get to the bottom of this without getting the authorities involved."

"You're talking about the Advanced Aerospace Threat Identification Program, with the Pentagon."

Gideon's eyes went wide, and he glanced to Lizzy

then to me. I shrugged and looked to Jae, who took on a whole new level of peculiar from the last time I saw her.

"Uh, no," he answered. "Meant something more along the lines of the Junction police department. Or a civil suit, given the thousands of dollars in damage to the man's crops. Which is where you two come in."

He passed back to me the thick manilla folder from across the desk.

I promptly passed the folder to Jae without a passing glance.

"Tell me you're joking..."

"Says's here," Jae said, eyeing the first page, "that Mr. Warner came to you a few days ago after large circles appeared in his crop of corn."

Gideon put his feet up on the desk. "That's right."

"Says he believed it to be the product of some teenagers belonging to a Mr. Jelsma."

He opened a packet of peanuts and popped a few in his mouth. Honey roasted, by the smell of it.

"Care to share?" I said, raising a brow.

He frowned and handed over the bag, which I obliged.

"Fran Jelsma, a widow with teenage triplets—"

Jae shuddered. "Oof, that had to hurt."

Gideon threw me a glance; I tossed him a shrug. "Anyway, apparently Warner had been trying to get her to sell her property to him for years. Cut right through his tracts of land but she refused to sell. I tried myself to broker a deal, but it was a no go. Warner threatened to get the city to invoke little-used eminent domain clauses to force her hand, but that was a no go too."

"Eminent domain?" I asked, popping a handful of peanuts in my mouth. "I thought only the government could take people's land for public use."

"Yeah, Fifth Amendment and all," Jae joined in before reciting: "'*No person shall be deprived of life, liberty, or property, without due process of law; nor shall private property be taken for public use, without just compensation.*'"

"Look at you two budding lawyers," Gideon said, motioning for his peanuts back.

I begrudgingly obliged. But not before throwing another handful in my mouth.

"Hey, let me in on that action!" Jae did the same, then passed along the half-drained bag to Gideon. He frowned, tossing it to his desk.

I said, "So back to Eminent Domain 101."

Jae nodded. "Yeah, I thought the government can only take private property if it is reasonably shown that said property will be used for public purpose only."

"Historically," Gideon said, "That's true, the clause having been used to take said private property for highways and other public works. But in 1954, in the landmark *Berman v. Parker* case, the Supreme Court expanded the definition of the public use Taking Clause to the Fifth Amendment to allow local governments broad authority to condemn so-called 'blighted areas' to improve them."

"And Jelsma's property is said blighted-area property?" asked Jae.

I snorted a laugh and shook my head. "Blighted area.

It's a nice-sized plot of woodland nestled next to the Grand River, is what it is."

"A *blighted*," Gideon corrected, "nice-sized plot of woodland nestled next to the Grand River."

"That his argument or yours?"

Gideon returned to the peanuts. "Point is, our client believes her sons destroyed his crops. Several thousand dollars' worth, too. And we need proof."

"What kind of proof?"

"Catching the knuckleheads in the act would be nice."

Jae snorted a laugh. "Yeah, right. Doesn't Farmer Joe—"

"Herb Warner..." Gideon corrected.

"Tomato, tomatoes. Farmer *Warner*, then—doesn't he have some fancy-shmancy video surveillance system or something?"

"This ain't Vegas."

"Or Magnum P.I.," I quipped.

Gideon stood. "I'm sure you'll figure something out. You always do, JP."

I joined him, so did Jae—with outstretched hand.

He eyed it, then looked at me.

"Believe it's only right to shake on things like this," she offered.

"Man to man?"

Gideon's eyes went wide before literally biting his tongue.

"I prefer to say human to human. But man to *woman* works, as the case may be, and if that's what you folks say in these parts—when the occasion arises."

Nearly busted a gut on that one, Gideon's cheeks throwing up a royal red flush that did my heart good. Not that I didn't like the kid. He was my boss, after all. Just sometimes got a little cocky.

And sometimes a Jae McCray is just what the doc ordered for such times.

He quickly took it. "Woman to man—err, man to woman then."

They shook and we left Gideon. With a shovel to find his way out of his hole.

Evening was turning out to be about as bad as the inside of that law office, though it smelled better. A thick blanket of Great Lakes humidity had settled on the place, amplifying the smells of summer. Fresh cut grass, flowering hyacinths, dog poop.

We took my car, an F-150 that still purred right, a throwback to my first car after Nam when Ford still knew what it was doing. Headed south down Main Street to Herb's farm, hoping to catch him before the sun set, get the lay of the land—literally, with his walk-through.

Drive was a quiet one, the two of us still getting our bearings with each other I supposed. Had been almost a decade, so it made sense. Did the catch-up since we'd last seen each other.

Me: working mostly bankruptcies and divorces and background checks after Jae left a brief stint under my employ before signing up freelance with O'Donnell; still single, not having married since Lynn passed, and still hadn't found the daughter I gave up after all these years; not missing the priesthood after leaving and hanging up my P.I. shingle.

Her: eventually hanging her own shingle after things didn't work in New York after things went south with the Mister-Who-Wasn't, right before her brief stint under my employ; worked freelance gigs for high-powered clients up and down the Left Coasts—East and West; same on the single front, not having bothered to get hitched after her future went up in flames, though had plenty of prospects.

Of course.

The conversation was a bit stilted, especially after we'd left things, so I was glad the drive south was quick.

Twenty minutes later I parked the truck on a freshly paved driveway in front of a beautiful two-story white farmhouse with black trim and sloping, peaked roofs, a large wrap-around front porch to die for lit with a dim-yellow glow. Oaks and maples older than the house itself towered above it. A weather-worn swing was anchored out front with a nice bed of flowers.

A GMC Denali flatbed was parked inside the open garage. One of those weird cars that made not a lick of sense. A luxury pickup? Who in their right mind would haul lumber or a cement mixer or bails of hay in one of those nonsense puff vehicles? Not as bad as the Cadillac Escalade EXT that went extinct in 2013, but still. Sort of like those even weirder Smart mini electric cars that wouldn't hold up in a downpour, let alone an accident. Why any farmer worth his salt would have one of them things was peculiar. Figured the guy more for a Chevy or Ford, and would have thought it was the missus's car, but Herb was a widow. To each his own I guessed. But it was clear the guy was doing well for himself, especially with the Bimmer sitting next to it.

Then there was the crown jewel of the property that made me roll my eyes.

A dog.

Was hollering something fierce as we drove the distance up the drive. Thing must've had a real set of ears on that head, it was going at it so much. Probably more bark than bite, the dog an itty-bitty white thing that was ten pounds wet. Definitely not your typical farm dog, that's for sure.

Probably woke the long-dead Warner ancestors buried in the family plots hanging off to the side, the farm having been in the family since the early days of Mill Creek Junction.

"Shut the hell up, Cupcake!" said Herb Warner storming through a screen door.

We turned to each other and mouthed *Cupcake?* with upturned brows.

The man stopped cold when he saw us approach, throwing up a nervous laugh. "Oh, hey, Father. Didn't know it was you who'd driven up."

"Herb," I said, clomping up the wood stairs painted forest green, "you know darn well I've been retired for a decade now. Something on your mind that you've got to confess?"

There was that nervous laugh again, Cupcake now firmly in his large arms and nestled against his blue overalls.

Now I laughed. "Just kidding, Herb. Johnny's fine."

I stuck out my hand; he took it with the one not

holding his little doggie. I gestured to Jae and made an introduction. They did the same.

"Gideon called us up and caught us up on your case. We're here to get the 411 from the man himself."

"Ahh, that's great!" Herb shoved Cupcake inside the house and closed the real front door of solid oak, the wood not able to fully contain the yapping.

"So, crop circles, huh?" Jae asked.

"Crop destruction, is what it is! And it was that Fran Jelsma and her boys, I just know it. Been frustrating my plans to expand—erm, bring good, healthy food to the people of Mill Creek and beyond for years."

Jae scoffed. "I bet…"

I threw her a glare. "Why don't you show us what you've got."

"It's just over here."

We walked across a nice green lawn smelling of fresh-cut grass and chewed the chaw, talking mostly about the crappy summer weather that was running his celery and onion crops.

Soon enough, just a we bit inside the corn field anchored due south and already reaching shoulder length, we came to the scene of the crime.

"There we are." Herb folded his massive arms across his generous gut and nodded toward the center. "You can see for yourself with the ladder over yonder."

Jae shrugged. "Don't mind if I do…"

She didn't, climbing up to the top and scanning the scene.

"Yep. Crop circle."

"Crop destruction," Herb reiterated again.

She hopped down and dusted off her Levis. "In the shape of a circle."

Herb threw up a dismissive hand. "Doesn't sing too well in the ears, crop circles, if you know what I mean."

I chuckled knowingly. Before I could start my own interrogation, Jae apparently had her own ideas.

"When did you say these appeared?" she asked.

"Day before yesterday."

"And did you see anything unusual? Pulsating lights, weird electrical surges in the homestead, Cupcake going wackadoodle?"

He frowned, crossing his arms. "No, I didn't. Cupcake was with me and made not a peep."

I held back my frown, wondering Jae's deal. She could be a bit much at times, and I usually gave her a long leash. But I might have to reign it in soon.

"What about any unexplained objects over the farm. Cylindrical like a Tic-Tac, or triangular like a block of Swiss cheese."

Herb snapped his fingers. "That's right. Almost forgot. I did awaken during the night and saw something right nutty!"

Jae leaned in, eyes wide and mouth open in a question.

"Hmm-hmm. That's right." Now Herb leaned in all serious like. "Little green men doing a conga line on my driveway!"

Took a beat until Jae knew what was what. Herb's belly laughs and backslapping me probably clued her in.

"Is this lady for real, Johnny?" he said wiping tears from his eyes.

Now I did frown. Unfortunately, probably.

I took a breath, then a beat, then said, "Come on, Jae. Let's go have a chat with Fran Jelsma."

"Cylindrical like a Tic-Tac, or triangular like a block of Swiss cheese!" Herb said from behind us as we hustled away. Right before he started with the belly laughs again.

Reaching the Ford, I opened the door for Jae. "I'd say that went well."

She smirked. "He's hiding something, I just know it."

I closed her door and left it alone. Then we drove the short distance to Fran's house, just the next property over.

Which was a much smaller ranch-style home. A single level thing of faded tan siding and a sagging roof. Looked like it needed a replacement five years ago, moss growing in spots and branches overhanging with threat. Darkness was really creeping in now, the sun setting and the massive trees butting against the property casting long shadows. A few cars sat on the lawn, so I was prepared for company. A mid-size John Deere was parked all cattywampus out front, too.

"If that don't scream black leather gloves," Jae said, nodding toward the tractor, "I don't know what does."

I grunted an agreement. Sure did scream OJ Simpson's saving grace. Yet, if the tractor don't fit, suppose we must acquit still rang true.

Parking, we ambled across the overgrown lawn, taking a quick side trip to the Deere. Was rusting pretty good, the blades covered in an orangish patina. Looked like it hadn't been used in a while. Hopping up to the cabin, I noticed the gas gauge was two-thirds spent. And the yard did have tire tracks, though couldn't make sense of them, whether they belonged to the Deere or two other cars. Could be our smoking gun, but maybe not.

We went to the front door and knocked. No dog this time, thank the good Lord above!

Fran answered with a frown, a rail-thin woman with stringy silver hair and a nightgown that sort of dripped off her slight frame. Folding her arms she offered almost a sneer. "So, he sent you after me, ehh? Thought my priest would be able to convince me to sell, did he?"

I gave Jae a sideways glance and smiled. "Hi, Fran. Nice to see you, too."

She offered nothing more, which was unlike the woman. We'd always had a cordial relationship, but the ice wall was a mile high.

Tread with caution.

"Uh, no, Fran, we're not here about your property."

Her arms fell to her side. "Oh, then what's this about?"

Jae went to answer when I grabbed her arm; her question caught in her throat.

Clearing my throat, I clarified: "We're here about Herb's property."

Those arms went back up again.

"And actually, your boys."

"My boys?" She twisted up her face and crossed her arms. "What they got to do with anything?"

"Are they here?" I asked, sidestepping the question. First rule of P.I.ing is always respond to a question with a question.

"No, what's this about?"

"Have you seen them today?"

She shrugged. "Sure. Breakfast, lunch, and dinner. Like any teenage boy."

I chuckled. "Ain't that the truth."

"This isn't about Herb, is it?"

"Why would you say that?" Jae asked now, following the rule I myself had taught her.

"Because that man has made my life a living hell the last year with trying to buy my property." She leaned in now, unfolding those spindly arms of hers and jabbing a finger in my chest. "But I ain't sellin'! You tell him that."

Fran backed off and shoved a stray lock of hair in place.

"Did your sons know about Warner's advances?" asked Jae.

Little soon for my taste, but saw no reason not to start the show.

Another shrug. "It was discussed."

"And they were irritated about it, weren't they? As irritated as you—angry, even?"

I eased in a stabilizing breath, trying not to glance Jae's way. We were approaching danger zone now. Could feel it, see it.

Steady...

"Not sure. You'd have to ask them."

"Oh, we will..."

I cleared my throat, wanting to move it in another direction.

I asked, "What about the other night. The one before last."

Fran huffed. "What of it?"

Was losing her, but there was one more thing I wanted to check.

"You see them, your sons?"

She nodded. "Sure did. Was our mom and sons' pizza night."

"Awe, how quaint," Jae said.

"All night?" I asked.

Another nod. "Was a Saw marathon, so yeah."

Didn't follow. "Saw marathon…"

"Yeah, you know. The movies."

"Movie?"

"All night?" Jae echoed, face twisted up.

"Yep. One through five."

Jae coughed, and sounded like a giggle was ready to poke through. But she held steady.

Another stabilizing breath, but I kept my eyes trained on Fran. "And they never left your side. Night before last?"

Fran frowned, checking her watch. "That's right. We through here? I've got Celebrity Jeopardy in five minutes, and frankly I don't I like where this conversation is going."

I put up my hands. "All through, Fran. Really appreciate the help. You have yourself a nice night now."

She left back inside, slamming the door behind.

We ambled back to the F-150, night having fully set in now.

"That went well," said Jae.

"I thought so. Got what we needed."

"Yeah, but we got nowhere on the sons."

I shrugged. "Sometimes nowhere is somewhere."

"You should print that on a T-shirt."

Jae leaned against the hood with a sigh. "So we know the sons couldn't have done the job. At least, according to dear ol' mama."

"Sounds that way."

"Now what?"

I frowned, taking in the view of the property—and the sky.

Lit up like a Christmas tree, it was. With all the trees and the darkness, the stars were especially bright in contrast.

"How about we head back to Warner's farm. Scope things out there, maybe plant our asses in his cornfields and wait for ET to show itself."

She pushed off from the hood with a grin. "What, like a stakeout?"

I chuckled. "You could call it that."

"You're on!"

Jae hopped inside the passenger's seat; I took the captain's chair and brought the beast to life.

Didn't take long before we were back at Herb's place and trucking across the lawn to a hill that rose above the fields at one end of the property. Got a good view of the rest of the land, in case the perp returned for round two on the crop circles front of things. Didn't bank on it, which was fine. Would give us a chance for some meditation time. Mull things over.

Nighttime creatures were out in force now, the crickets and katydids playing their tunes. Heard some rustling in the corn rows as we trudged up the berm too, hoping it wasn't something that would eat us. The rancid scent of skunk reassured us at one level, and put us on alert on another. Last thing either of us wanted was to get sprayed!

Rustling went away and we plopped ourselves down on the berm after clearing away dry weeds and grass. Smelled of earth and decay, followed by curious twin scents of woodsmoke and cooking oil.

Stretching out in her Levis and slinging a leg over the other, those boots sticking toward the open sky above, Jae sighed with contentment. "Tell you what, a girl could get used to this kind of view."

Had to agree, joining her and stretching out for the night watch, and the view.

"I would have thought the view was better out your way in that small town of yours."

She scoffed. "Not with Vegas a klick down the road."

"Suppose that's true."

We stared up at the sea of stars, making out some distant planets blinking at us caught in the riptide of the Milky Way Galaxy. Or some satellite junking up space.

Silence settled between us, but not around us. All manner of bugs started continuing their chorus, joined by tree frogs and the distant rush of the highway a klick farther south. A cool breeze from Lake Michigan made things bearable, the trace scents of that cooking oil and woodsmoke again telling me someone had pitched a tent in the woods close to the Junction. Probably the Jelsma boys waiting for their moment to strike.

"I saw one once, you know," Jae said without an ounce of equivocation—or shame—the woman staring up into the night sky with one end of her mouth curling upward.

Then it dawned.

"You mean a—" I paused, choosing my words.

She giggled in the meantime. "Yeah, I do. A flying saucer."

I whistled, not expecting that in the slightest.

Clearing my throat, not wanting that to be my first response—or only—I said, "Back in Cave Creek? You said strange stuff was brewing in those parts."

She took in a measured breath and leaned back on her hands, getting all comfortable like.

"Looked like a triangle, with three spotlights at each of the three vertices. A red one shone round and bright, smack dab in the center."

I hummed. "Like a bullseye."

She turned to me with a smile. "That's right. Cast a wicked crimson glow across the landscape, too, as it hovered there. Silent, unmoving. As if it wasn't even there."

I'd known Jae clear back into her childhood. Her daddy was part of a local cohort of ministers who got together to commiserate. She had been a teenager when I was still a young pup in ministry, having gone into the priesthood after my wife passed and I gave up our daughter at a fire station. I was in my thirties, so it didn't seem right—but man, Jae was a looker back then in the Nineties.

Just like now...

I gave her a glance, her face still transfixed at the

stars, the sliver moonlight falling just right on her face in a way that cast her as a porcelain doll.

She shifted, so I snapped my head back to the heavens as well, then took a breath to steady myself, getting my head screwed back on right.

Anyway, she was also a firecracker, to be sure. Sometimes given over to theatrics and antics that were a bit more than some could handle. Had a real attitude, too, knowing who she was and what she wanted.

But never in all my years had I known her to lie. Truth-telling was Jael McCray's way. Sometimes to a fault, and sometimes in a way that made others uncomfortable.

So to hear her tell this tale...to tell her truth, as they say nowadays—it was unnerving. Was waiting for her to toss her head back in one of her trademark snorty laughs that got me and tease me for being so gullible.

That never came. Not the laughter, not the good-hearted tease.

Just kept staring up into the sky so that I didn't know what to believe.

"You think I'm crazy," Jae finally said. "Don't you?"

I shifted on the hard berm, slinging a leg over the other and not breaking contact with the world above.

"Not crazy..."

She laughed. "Then a lunatic."

I turned to her now. "No, it's just—"

"No, no, no. It's alright. I get that a lot."

"Look, I don't discount what you saw."

"But..."

"But, maybe it was some Air Force tech on display."

"In the Junction? Come on."

Now that threw me for a loop. Assumed she was talking about her time out in Nevada, where I knew there were a few Air Force bases nearby. Not Michigan. Well, not any to speak of anyway, just a smattering of National Guards bases that didn't amount to much. So to think something like she described had visited her, in Mill Creek Junction, probably twenty years ago—boy, that was a turn.

Jae turned to me now, a smile playing across her face and her deep brown eyes on fire. "So, Father—"

"Father…" I laughed nervously. "That was a long time ago."

"So you've said. I'd love to know what you think they are. No chance of extraterrestrial life out there?"

She pointed toward the sea of diamonds, eyes still locked on me.

I shrugged. "Is there a chance? Sure. Anything's possible. But of course that would mean Jesus Christ himself had created them. Since, you know, all things were created in, through, and for him. As the Apostle Paul says in the Book of Colossians."

"Of course."

"And if they had free will, they would need a Savior —Jesus Christ himself, given they would inevitably rebel against God and turn to their own way."

"Naturally."

"Yet that would mean a second incarnation, Jesus visiting another planet in alien form—which doesn't seem right."

"Hmm-mm."

I turned to her, Jae having one hand under her chin and the other draped across her knee. Looking like she was enjoying seeing me squirm.

"You're enjoying this, aren't you?"

"Hmm-mm," Jae said with a giggle. I joined her with a chuckle.

Silence filled the space between us.

Until there wasn't.

"Wait..." I said, standing up.

"You hear that?" said Jae, joining me.

"Sure do."

"A low hum with a *thwap-thwap-thwap*ing?"

I cocked my head, staring out into the dead of night. "Sounds about right?"

We stood there listening, intuiting, discerning what it was that had joined us that night.

Heart was racing real good now, too. And breath was picking up along with a ping of adrenaline to the brain that branched into the fight-or-flight choices that inevitably unfold during those times.

Especially after Jae's stories about UFOs and what not. Even glanced up into the night sky, half expecting to glimpse the triangle lights and red orb Jae swore she saw. Nothing but the full moon and sea of stars.

Jae sighed and moaned with disappointment. "Only a tractor, if I reckon right."

"You think?" I took a step, straining my eyes toward the sound now I knew was coming from the ground, not from the sky above.

She nailed it. Sounded exactly like a tractor. Only—

"Who would be driving a tractor," Jae said, "this late at night on Warner's farm?"

I turned to her with a frown. "Exactly. Come on. Let's check it out."

We raced down the berm and into the corn, the stalks throwing up all kinds of vegetative smells and slapping us in the face with leaves. Was tricky navigating the maze of cornstalks, but we made for the sound of the grunting tractor. That was our True North.

Almost there now, the sound right on top of us. Until—

We popped out into a field of flattened corn, those vegetative smells on top of earthy manure being thrown up at us on top of the grumbly rumbly John Deere circling the joint in the full silver moonlight. Looked like a cousin to the one we'd seen at Fran's house. Perhaps even the same one.

"Let's see if we can rustle up the intruder," Jae said. "OK-Corral style."

"You'd know best."

We padded along the periphery of the flattened circle, going our separate ways to sneak up on the perp. Brought my phone out now and flipped the camera on, capturing video of the tractor grunting along the circular course and readying for our hidey-ho. Figured it could be useful if it came to a trial.

The Deere grunted to a sputtering halt, apparently finished with its work of art. Wondered how they got it into the field, but looked a little like what we had glimpsed at Fran's. Not a good look. In this case, the glove seemed to fit.

Jae and I came from our separate ways making for the tractor, the door opening and a figure lumbering down the stairs whispering a curse.

Sort of wished I'd brought my Heckler & Koch pistol with me. Never knew when cold, hard steel would be in order.

"Freeze!" I heard up ahead, another round of curses from a man joining Jae's shout.

Looked like she brought the steel for the both of us.

I hustled now, not knowing what the firecracker might do. On my approach I heard Jae curse, "Son of a monkey's uncle!"

Coming up behind the perp, I saw her lower her weapon and mutter another curse. Standing before her was a large man with his hands up in shorts and a T-shirt.

And a yapping dog in the carriage.

"Herb?" I asked with confusion.

He turned around, hands still raised.

Sure enough. Herb Warner, Cupcake really going at it now. Thankfully from inside the Deere.

"What in the blazes are you doing out here?"

"Cutting crop circles, I reckon," said Jae. "You can put your hands down now, by the way. I won't blow your head off. Yet..."

He obliged, one hand going to the back of his head as a chuckle slipped through lips grinning sheepishly. "Well, this sure is awkward."

I frowned. "I'd say. Is Jae right, you were the perp all this time?"

Silence was all I got, the man kicking a stray stone.

Whether from embarrassment or from getting caught, it wasn't clear.

"Why? What were you thinking?"

Herb shrugged. "Needed the money."

Jae said, "So you framed your neighbor, then decided to sue her for damages?"

I added, "On top of trying to wrench her property from her under shady legal mumbo jumbo—about the long and short of it?"

He shrugged again, saying nothing more.

Had half a mind to slug the sonofagun then and there. Instead, I took Jae by the arm. "I think we're through here."

And we were. Nothing more to see, nothing more to do. But boy would Gideon get an earful.

"I'll come clean with Gideon," Herb called out as we sauntered across the flattened corn. "I'll make it right."

"You better believe you will..." I muttered.

I dropped Jae off at the local Holiday Inn and returned home for some shut-eye. We met back at Gideon's law firm the next morning after breakfast to give him the full report.

Gideon and his crew were waiting for us with two packages. He handed me a large envelope, then another to Jae. Heavy and stuffed to the brim with something that felt like bricks.

"What's this?" I asked, afraid to look inside.

"Your earnings."

"From Herb?" asked Jae, taking a peek inside.

"That's right."

"But we didn't do anything. Aside from solving the case for Fran's sake, I suppose."

"Fair is fair. Besides, Herb felt he should pay up after what went down."

That was surprising. "He told you?"

Gideon nodded, saying nothing more.

"You mean," Jae said, "He thought he should pay hush money."

He remained silent.

I opened the envelope and startled. "What, in cash?"

"Herb doesn't believe in banks. Wanted to pay you in cash. Safer that way, too, with the nature of the case and all."

I nodded, the metallic scent of a whole lot of Benjamins flaring up the gullet of the yellow envelope, my eyes growing large at the sight down inside.

A whistle escaped Jae's parted lips as she took in her own sight. "Ten grand a piece?"

Gideon nodded. "Ten grand. Don't spend it all in one place!"

We joined him in a laugh.

"A drink sure would be nice to celebrate, though," Jae said.

The room went still, quiet. Uncomfortably so after what she shared about her sobriety.

"I'm kidding!" she said with a giggle. "Jeez Louise. Tough crowd."

Reggie and Lizzy laughed uncomfortably. Gideon said nothing, turning to me for help.

To which I replied, "How about meatloaf piled high with Mary's potatoes, green beans stacked on the side and some sweet tea. Down at Millie's on Main. For old time's sake."

Jae closed the envelope and tucked it under her arm, then pushed a stray lock of that ginger hair of hers behind an ear. "I'd like that."

Me too.

Welcome to a new story world inspired by such fictional towns as John Grisham's Clanton, Mississippi, and Stephen King's Castle Rock, Maine.

Get to know this world one character, one setting, one event and situation at a time. You're sure to find some of your own story in theirs, while being entertained and inspired for the journey.

Visit www.millcreekjunction.com for more details about the world and a list of short and long-form fiction, following the lives of real people living life and exploring faith, with new stories each week.

Building a relationship with my readers is one of my all-time favorite joys of writing! Once in a while I like to send out a newsletter with giveaways, free stories, pre-release content, updates on new books, and other bits on my stories.

Join my insider's group for updates, giveaways, and your free novel—a full-length action-adventure story in my *Order of Thaddeus* thriller series. Just tell me where to send it.

Follow this link to subscribe:
www.jabouma.com/free

Martyrs Bones: Short Story Collection 2

***Ichthus Chronicles* Sci-Fi Apocalyptic Series**

Apostasy Rising / Season 1, Episode 1

Apostasy Rising / Season 1, Episode 2

Apostasy Rising / Season 1, Episode 3

Apostasy Rising / Season 1, Episode 4

Apostasy Rising / Full Season 1 (Episodes 1 to 4)

Apocalypse Rising / Season 2, Episode 1

Apocalypse Rising / Season 2, Episode 2

Apocalypse Rising / Season 2, Episode 3

Apocalypse Rising / Season 2, Episode 4

Apocalypse Rising / Full Season 2 (Episodes 1 to 4)

***Faith Reimagined* Spiritual Coming-of-Age Series**

A Reimagined Faith • Book 1

A Rediscovered Faith • Book 2

A Ruined Faith • Book 3 (2022)

A Resurrected Faith • Book 4 (2023)

***Mill Creek Junction* Short Story Series**

Get all the latest short stories at: www.millcreekjunction.com

Find all of my latest book releases at: www.jabouma.com

ABOUT THE AUTHOR

J. A. Bouma believes nobody should have to read bad religious fiction—whether it's cheesy plots with pat answers or misrepresentations of the Christian faith and the Bible. So he wants to do something about it by telling compelling, propulsive stories that thrill as much as inspire, while offering a dose of insight along the way.

As a former congressional staffer and pastor, and award-nominated bestselling author of over forty religious fiction and nonfiction books, he blends a love for ideas and adventure, exploration and discovery, thrill and thought. With graduate degrees in Christian thought and the Bible, and armed with a voracious appetite for most mainstream genres, he tells stories you'll read with abandon and recommend with pride—exploring the tension of faith and doubt, spirituality and culture, belief and practice, and the gritty drama that is our collective pilgrim story.

When not putting fingers to keyboard, he loves vintage jazz vinyl, a glass of Malbec, and an epic read—preferably together. He lives in Grand Rapids with his wife, two kiddos, and rambunctious boxer-pug-terrier.

www.jabouma.com • jeremy@jabouma.com

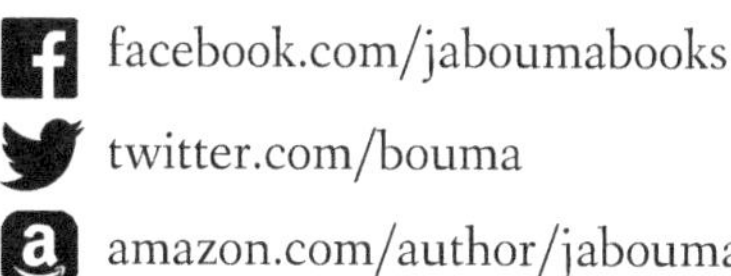

facebook.com/jaboumabooks
twitter.com/bouma
amazon.com/author/jabouma